THE ANCIENT OMEN

Elijah Creek & The Armor of God #2

The Ancient Omen

Lena Wood

Standard
PUBLISHING
Bringing The Word to Life™

Project editor: Lindsay Black
Content editor: Amy Beveridge
Copy editor: Lynn Lusby Pratt
Cover and interior design: Robert Glover
Cover photography: Robert Glover
Cover oil paintings: Lena Wood
Map illustration: Daniel Armstrong
Scripture taken from the HOLY BIBLE, NEW INTERNATIONAL
VERSION®. NIV®. Copyright © 1973, 1978, 1984 by International
Bible Society. Used by permission of Zondervan. All rights reserved.

Library of Congress Cataloging-in-Publication Data

Wood, Lena, 1950-
    The ancient omen / Lena Wood.
        p. cm. -- (Elijah Creek & the armor of God ; bk. 2)
    Summary: The discovery of the belt of truth draws Elijah and his friends
back into the forbidden haunts of Telanoo, where they discover an old mystery
which leads Elijah into trouble--and new understandings of his relationship
with God.
    ISBN 0-7847-1590-4 (pbk.)
    [1. Christian life--Fiction. 2. Friendship--Fiction.] I. Title.
 II. Series: Wood, Lena, 1950-   . Elijah Creek & the armor of God ; bk. 2.
PZ7.W84973An 2005
[Fic]--dc22

                                                    2004010155

                        ISBN 0-7847-1590-4

  01 00 09 08 07 06 05   9 8 7 6 5 4 3 2 1

to **Wendell** *and* **Gloria** *and* **The Circle,**
who fight for me in prayer

Deepest appreciation to:
Zach Hudson, Alonzo Rutledge, *and*
Junwen (Jennifer) Pan, *cover models*
Dan Dyke, *Old Testament adviser*
Fort Mitchell Church,
for unwavering encouragement

&

The Ancient Truth, *still speaking*

Chapter 1

THERE we were under the Bone Tree with a muddy sack we'd just dug out of Devil's Cranium. The sunny day Reece had prayed for suddenly turned blustery and cold. Wind cut like razors across that hill and right through our jackets. We kept low to the ground on our hands and knees around the spot where the metal detector had beeped.

Mei put on plastic gloves—like we'd decided to do when handling the artifacts—as if we were investigating a crime. We held our breaths as Mei slowly reached into the sack. Something small and round fell out. It was a broken compass.

Weeks before, we'd found the helmet and right arm of the armor of God, which had long ago been buried in the basement of Old Pilgrim Church, and which old Stan Dowland had dug up and re-buried near the cemetery. The rest of it was still at large. We had ourselves a mystery involving two ancient relics, maybe worth a fortune. But thanks to my stupidity we had lost them, with little hope of ever finding them again. Only a thousand-year-old scrap of chain mail remained, and it was now in the hands of a scientist in Chicago by the name of Stallard.

It was clear that this was a quest, and that all of us—but especially me, Elijah Creek—had been chosen for it. Reece came to that conclusion after I told her about my night alone in The Cedars when a Bible verse came ringing inside my head: *Put on the full armor of God.* That kind of thing had never happened to me before.

So I became head of this operation.

The rest of the group on the quest were Reece and her Japanese friend Mei, my cousin Robbie, and Skid. I don't mind saying I wasn't thrilled about letting Skid into our group. But he was useful. He found Stanford Dowland, the key to our quest; and Skid made connections with Dr. Stallard, who advised us to keep quiet about the armor until further notice. Skid was convinced the scientist could be trusted.

Mei laid the compass in her palm and we all leaned in. It was rusty and the glass was shattered and mostly gone.

"Is that it?" Skid asked. "That's no relic."

"I thought you said you felt a belt in there," Robbie snipped.

Reece was still holding the sack. "It's in here. Has to be. Get it out, Mei."

Mei laid the compass down and looked in the sack again.

"It is a belt!" she said.

The wind swept over us, building as it blew across the dead meadows of Telanoo. We braced ourselves against it and studied the belt. It didn't look ancient, but it wasn't modern either. It was a leather strip about the width of your hand. The buckle was strange: a metal plate with rough lumps and lines, like it had been hammered into shape. On either side of the buckle was faded tapestry material.

"Those designs, do they look Indian to you?" I asked.

"Maybe African," said Mei, "or from the Middle East."

Odd-shaped pieces of metal were strung around the back of the belt on leather laces.

"Yes!" Reece looked at it lovingly. Her breathing was uneven. I thought she might faint.

"You okay?" I asked.

"We will find all of it," she said with conviction. "It may take a while, but we will find the whole armor of God."

For a long time she knelt over the belt, easing the dust and dirt off. "*Aletheia,*" she whispered excitedly.

Skid repeated it, and they looked at each other across the dig, their eyes all glittery. *Skid and Reece and their blasted secret bond!*

"What?" I asked, scooting over beside her. "You see something?"

"Truth." Reece smiled at me. "The belt should say *aletheia,* which is 'truth' in Greek."

"How do you know that?" I asked.

"The other two pieces had Greek engravings, so I looked up all the words from Ephesians chapter six that describe the armor."

Reece's leg was killing her and she needed to stand. She handed the belt back to Mei, and I helped her up. We all examined the belt, hoping to see the same kind of letters we'd seen on the other pieces: the helmet of *soterion,* or "salvation," and the right arm piece engraved with the word *koinonia,* "fellowship."

Mei picked away the mud caked on the buckle. "Is this a word . . . or a symbol?"

"It has to be the belt of truth!" Reece cried.

Skid tried to be encouraging. "Does it have to have the word on it?"

Reece said, "It should. Truth doesn't hide."

Huge gusts of wind slammed into the hill, stronger with each slam. The last one almost knocked us over. Mother Nature had taken up bowling and we were the pins.

"We gotta get out of here!" I yelled over the wind. "C'mon!" Getting Reece over the rocks and across the rutted terrain of Telanoo was going to take a while.

Time and time again I'd asked about who owned this land northeast of the camp. Once Dad said, "Oh, it's probably part of the Morgan farm." Another time he said, "Maybe Old Pilgrim Church owns it." Then another time, "Could be part of Council Cliffs State Park. I'm not sure, Elijah." I'd asked others and gotten the same runaround. Bo, the camp activities and security director said, "There's nothing back there." Mrs. Horstley who does office work at camp said, "Well, I don't really know, hon, but it couldn't be near as pretty and nice as the campgrounds. If you see 'No Trespassing' signs back there, you should stay out." Never a real answer. There were no signs, nothing to keep me out or fight against my crazy curiosity to prowl about whenever I had the chance.

The five of us made the long hike back to the golf cart in good time. Reece walked much better on the way out than she had on the way in. Maybe it was the excitement of finding another piece of the armor. We loaded ourselves and our gear into the golf cart. As we zipped along the paved path through Owl Woods, we talked about where to take our treasure for a closer look. Once in plain sight of the camp buildings, it hit me: the camp was busy on all fronts today. I yelled above the roar of the wind and the cart's motor, "We've got to find another place! Camp's busting at the seams. High school retreat in the front cabins, historical meeting at the lodge, Pioneer Days for middle schoolers at the shelter house. And . . . oh no . . ."

A dead serious look must have washed over my face.

"Elijah! What's wrong?" Reece asked.

"The Mad River Boys are coming later on. I just remembered."

"Mad River Boys?" Reece asked.

"From the boys' ranch upstate. A reform school. Big trouble! Dad has to put them in the back cabins!"

We burst out of the shelter of the woods into the wintry blast again. Skid tucked the sack into his black suede jacket, buttoning it up to his neck.

Reece and Mei were shivering but not complaining. The smell of snow was in the air. I went full throttle around the lake trail toward home. "I'll let you out at my house. You guys scope out the situation there while I drop off the cart."

We unloaded the metal detector and canteens at the front porch. "Keep the belt hidden, Skid," I reminded. "My sisters are around. And don't lose that compass. It may be a clue."

I sped to the maintenance building and slammed on the brakes, skidding to a stop. Tossing the keys onto the wall hook by the sign-out board, I dashed back to the house. While the others stood in the entryway, I cased the place. Straight ahead in the kitchen, Mom was glued to the phone while unloading groceries. The twins, Nori and Stacy, were acting like typical four-year-olds—not a good thing since they were almost seven. They'd built a fort with blankets and couch cushions in the living room, dragging every last baby doll and piece of toy furniture downstairs from their room. In about three minutes they'd be tired of it and on to something else, with the house a wreck and Mom saying, "Elijah, honey, can you give me a hand? The girls have over-extended themselves."

There'd be no privacy with them bored and on the loose—not even in my room with the door locked. Call me crazy, but I wouldn't be shocked if it turned out the twins had surveillance equipment in my room. Maybe they crawl through the heat ducts and spy on me. I swear, I can tiptoe down to get a snack in the kitchen, and in the three-fourths of a minute it takes me to throw a slice of ham on bread and get back to my room, they've sacked it, or have flattened themselves under my bed pillows or behind my camping gear in the closet. I swear they can hide out in my room for days without food or water. When I complain, Mom always pats my face and says, "It's because they admire you, Elijah," to which I usually say, "Why can't they admire me from afar . . . like Siberia?"

"This won't work," I said to Robbie. "What about your place—in the attic?"

We sat around the table in our log kitchen, acting casual and drinking hot chocolate while Robbie called his mom to come pick us up. I didn't get roped into cleaning up the twins' mess only because I had company.

"She'll be here in twenty minutes," said Robbie.

Mom said, "Then why don't you take off your coats and get comfortable?"

We said we were still cold.

Chapter 2

WE rode along, listening to classical music playing on the radio under Aunt Grace's small talk. She asked in a real mommy voice, "Did you kids find any buried treasure with the metal detector?" (I should say here that if you're ever on a quest for ancient treasure, there's no need to hide it from your parents. They'll think you're playing a kid game and go right along.)

Robbie said, "Yeah, we found a broken compass." (I should also say that he didn't tell her about the belt of truth because the five of us had made a pact of secrecy. What I mean is, talking about plain old priceless buried treasure is one thing; spilling the beans about the armor of God is another.)

Aunt Grace said, "Better luck next time."

We grinned at each other secretly.

Reece and Mei had never been to The Castle, as it's called around town. It's an 1800s Victorian-style home, on some historical register because it's the twenty-first oldest house in the state. A world-traveling politician built it, with imported Italian marble for the fireplace and entry floor, and teakwood paneling from India for the dining room. I never did understand the big deal about having all that fancy-schmancy stone and wood. Our log house is every bit as nice. And nothing is more awesome than the huge creek-stone fireplace at the Camp

Mudj lodge. Aunt Grace and Uncle Dorian were constantly telling Mom and Dad all about the future "Wingate Bed and Breakfast and Tea Room."

To be honest, they hadn't made much progress. The white clapboard siding was all chipped, the little round window in the tower was cracked and boarded up, and the left side of the porch sagged like an old mattress.

Mei flipped over the house. "This is so beautiful. And so big!"

"It was one of the very first houses in Magdeline," Aunt Grace said proudly. "We rescued it from destruction." She dragged us around to every room, showing Reece and Mei her antiques and paintings. I'd heard it all before. Mei seemed interested, but she was always so polite, you couldn't tell what she really felt. Reece was polite too, but she was like me: in a big rush to get to the attic.

"Anyone feel like lasagna?" asked Aunt Grace. "I can have some warmed up in half an hour."

"That'd be great! We'll be in the attic," I said, pulling Reece toward the stairs.

Aunt Grace snickered. "Secret club? Private meeting?"

"We're too old for secret clubs," I said.

I led the way to the second floor, past Robbie's room, to a set of narrow steps going straight up to the attic. We closed the door behind us and turned on the one lone lightbulb overhead. It was creepy all right, but Robbie had cleared a place for hanging out in the middle of all the clutter. His parents were always going nuts antique shopping and talking with historians and decorators, so we were usually left alone.

There are clawing noises in the attic wall sometimes—not skittery mouse scratches you might hear in your own house—but big sounds. And the *thunk*ing noises on the roof at night! Robbie and I figured it was probably raccoons jumping onto the roof from a big tree behind the house. But if you're trying to sleep up there, it sounds more like Kodiak bears dropping from aircraft.

The attic had an old velvet couch waiting to be reupholstered. There was an oriental screen and an antique kitchen cabinet where we kept books and a radio. Mannequins—left over from Aunt Grace's short career at Mitts Bros. Department Store, right before it went out of business—reached out from the dark corners with stiff arms and blank stares. A rocking chair faced the one window. A couple of years ago, I'd joked to Robbie, "One of these days you're going to come up here at midnight and whip that chair around and have *Psycho*'s old Mrs. Bates herself, all dried up and gaping at you."

Robbie always said that watching so many old, scary movies was going to warp me. To prove his point, he fixed up a skinny dummy with a shabby brown dress and beige shawl. She had a bleach bottle head, a wig, and some hands from one of the mannequins. A magazine picture of Eleanor Roosevelt with the eyes blacked out was her face. Robbie went to a ridiculous amount of work for it not to scare me, so I pretended it did.

Movies weren't the problem. To be honest, I hadn't been the same since meeting Stan Dowland. After the old church burned down, and after his demon dog Salem came after us, it preyed on my mind what kind of revenge Dowland might be planning next. People tend not to like you after you hack up their pets, even though it was a clear case of self-defense, and I'd say that in a court of law.

The girls sat on the velvet couch with the burlap sack in their laps. We guys gathered around on the floor. Mei put on the plastic gloves again, took out the compass, placed it on her palm, and studied it. "It is not so old, I think. Maybe this is glue." Moving it in front of our eyes, she showed us the clear hard stuff which stuck the needle to its face. We each examined the compass without touching it.

"It looks like someone broke the glass and glued down the needle to keep it pointing in one direction," Robbie said.

"You think Dowland did it?" Skid asked.

"Who else?" I said. "He buried the armor."

"But why?" Mei asked, examining the back of the compass.

"Maybe it points to where the next piece is buried," Reece said excitedly. Suddenly her face dropped. "Oh no . . . "

"Oh no!" Mei repeated. "When I opened the sack, the compass fell out! We don't know the way it pointed when it was in the ground!"

"Rats!" Robbie said. "Another clue lost!"

Mei's small eyes got wide. "I made the mistake?"

"Mei, it's okay." Reece smiled. "*Daijoubu.*"

"Yeah," I said. "Anyone pulling the bag out would have flipped the compass. That can't be the answer."

Mei looked closely at the compass. "The needle is glued to ENE. What does that mean?"

"East-northeast," I said.

Skid turned to me. "Hey, Elijah, from there at the Bone Tree, where we were standing, which way was east-northeast?"

"I don't know," I admitted. I tried to reason it out. "Wind usually comes from the west . . . but it was crazy up there, whipping at us from everywhere. Dad's map of the camp doesn't show Telanoo either. . . . Man, I should have paid attention to the sun!" I said, angry at myself.

Skid said, "We're cool. We'll figure this out, Creek."

He and I cracked fists in a friendly way. I wasn't totally convinced that Skid was as cool as everyone gave him credit for, but it was getting easier to be around him.

"The library!" chirped Robbie. "We can find land plats there."

"Land plats?" I asked.

"Maps showing where the borders are, record of ownership, and topography: hills and creeks and roads."

"*Record of ownership?* You mean we can find out who owns Telanoo from the library?" I thumped him. "Why didn't you tell me before? I've been wanting to know that forever!"

He frowned. "Sorry!"

"Hey, Wingate, pretty smart about the land plats," Skid said. "How'd you know that?"

"When my parents were looking to buy The Castle, they dragged me all over creation: real estate offices and libraries and—hey, wait a minute!" Robbie interrupted himself and shot me a look. "Why'd you thump me? You *never* asked me who owned Telanoo!"

"I didn't?"

"No!" Robbie punched my arm.

"Ouch!" I said, as if he'd really hurt me.

"Wimp!" he got up and ran behind the couch to escape the punch he knew was coming.

All of a sudden we were seven years old again. "Coming through!" I leaped over the couch. The girls squealed and ducked. I got Robbie in a headlock and knuckled his fuzzy scalp. "Dork!" I said.

I let go, dodged his next punch, knocking Mrs. Bates out of the rocker and onto her face.

"Toad!" He threw a hatbox at me and caught me on the shoulder. I caught it before it fell, lobbed it back, and followed with a wad of artificial flowers. We could have gone on another hour, but Reece and Mei were giving us superior girl looks.

Chapter 3

BY the time we'd finished off Aunt Grace's leftover lasagna and took off for the library, a few blocks from The Castle, it was dark and spitting snow. I walked ahead of the others, thinking. The whole armor of God idea still puzzled me. *If there is a God, why would he hide his armor in the first place? I can't speak for him personally, but I wouldn't stash it here of all places.*

Magdeline was Nowheresville, U.S.A. It had only one main street, with a library, two banks, an antique mall, a courthouse, a drugstore with an old-fashioned soda fountain, and a few other places, like law offices. A little side street in the business district had a few more shops and the news office; that was about it. Mom said it had "charm" and "a ton of potential." Frankly, the town wasn't much without Camp Mudjokivi.

Skid and Mei found us a table next to the magazine rack and waited for Robbie to get the book. He ran up to the counter, trying to make his short neck longer, to look official. Reece and I stood on either side of him. Mrs. Otto's big eyes had landed on us the moment we came bursting in from the cold. She came tromping out from behind her desk in the back room. "Ten minutes to closing!"

Magdeline's head librarian was a squat lady with gray-brown hair and a flat face. Thick glasses made her eyes un-human and large. Think lemur, and you'd be close.

"Current land plats around Camp Mudjokivi, please," Robbie said.

She peered at us suspiciously, glancing over at Skid and Mei to get a head count. I could hear her alarm bells going off. Here it was closing time and five eighth-graders come racing in for no good reason, right before Thanksgiving when everyone else was out Christmas shopping. I personally never came into the library, except once or twice to get books on Indians and weapons. Skid—wearing his usual black, gang-type getup—looked like he'd never cracked a book in his life. She thought we were up to no good. "That will be a reference book, which means you can't take it out of the library."

"It's for a school project," I explained to put her at ease.

Reece shot me a look, then leaned in and went eye-to-lemur-eye with Mrs. Otto. "Actually, that's a big lie, ma'am. The truth is," she whispered dramatically, "we're trying to find ancient secret treasures in the forbidden land behind the camp."

Reece got uptight about always telling people the exact truth, even though we were sworn to secrecy. It was a problem—for me anyway—knowing what to say and not say.

Mrs. Otto smiled sweetly at Reece and said, "I see. Just a minute." She scowled at me, pivoted, and tromped into the back room again.

I nudged Robbie and whispered, "I'm impressed. You are king of the nerds."

"And you're a primitive savage Indian," he teased back.

He knows it gets my goat, calling the Indians primitive, because Creeks were one of the Five Civilized Tribes, and I may be part Creek.

I was ready to punch him again when Reece turned to me and practically snarled, "Elijah! You don't *lie* when you're trying to find out about the belt of *truth,* for Heaven's sake!" She heaved a sigh and shuddered like I had no clue about anything. Then she actually said it: "You have no idea how the universe works, do you?"

How do you answer a question like that?

Mrs. Otto came back with a book the size of a football field. "You may sit at this table." She pointed at one closest to the desk. "Eight minutes!"

"But our friends are over there." I thumbed in the direction of Mei and Skid.

Reece ignored me and said, "Yes ma'am, we'll sit here. Thank you very much." They swapped smiles again.

You might think that people are nice to Reece just because they feel sorry for her. But the truth is—and I'm thinking this right after she insulted me, so you know I'm being objective—how can you not like her? She's got guts and she's pretty, and she doesn't jabber on and giggle all the time. I like to compare people to animals, but Reece is hard to nail down. She's kind of like a little yellow canary with a sharp beak.

After all the wondering and asking, I was antsy to find out who owned Telanoo. Each page of the big book was nothing but curvy lines showing creeks and roads, straight dotted lines showing boundaries, numbers like S50W 700p, and little paragraphs like: Edmund Blanchet to Cadwallader Young D 046, 27 June, 1939—to show who owned what and when.

Camp Mudj and the surrounding areas were on page 21. I figured Owl Woods and Devil's Cranium would be easy to spot, but they weren't.

We hovered over the map while Robbie's busy finger traced across it. He's great with maps. The type was so small only he could read it. "Okay, here's the camp lake."

"Elijah, you know the land best," Skid said. "Where's Devil's Cranium from there?"

"I want to know who owns Telanoo first," I said.

"I can't make anything out," said Robbie. "Look at all these paragraphs. It'll take an hour to read every one, and we only have eight minutes."

"Six minutes!" snipped Mrs. Otto from behind her big desk.

His finger stopped. "Hold on! Remember that S-shaped creek where you hid the helmet and arm piece, and where Mr. Dowland stole them back? This looks like it!"

"Shhh!" hissed Mrs. Otto, even though we were the only ones in the library.

"Sorry," whispered Reece, and smiled.

"Yeah, but there were lots of curves, remember?" I said quietly.

He studied it a little more. "No, I think this is the one. We've found the first landmark."

We cheered in a whispery way.

"Hurry!" Reece said.

Robbie dug his finger into the page excitedly. "So . . . go a little north, away from the camp . . . there . . . I think that's Devil's Cranium."

Out of the blue Reece said, "The truth will set you free."

We all looked at her.

"'You will know the truth, and the truth will set you free.'" She grinned at me, but she was using that serious tone she uses when she quotes the Bible.

"Why'd you say that?" I asked.

She shrugged. "I don't know. It just popped into my mind."

I went back to looking at the map. I never know how to take Reece when she talks Bible.

Robbie drew a straight line with his finger. "There's Council Cliffs State Park."

"Looks like the line points toward Hermits' Cave," I said, surprised.

We argued over which was more east or northeast until the librarian shushed us again. "Two minutes!"

"We should have brought the compass and laid it right on the map," said Skid.

"Let's make a copy and take it back," Robbie suggested.

Mei quietly asked, "Where is the old broken house?"

"Oh yeah, the ruin," said Reece.

"But we didn't find anything there," I reminded her.

Robbie's finger moved in a straight line back toward Devil's Cranium. "It was at the far end of that big meadow. The ruin would be in a wide place with no landmarks."

Sure enough, the meadow lay directly east-northeast, between Devil's Cranium and the park.

"You mean the compass would have led us back to the ruin?" Reece asked.

This was bad news. "We've already been over that place," I said.

"Maybe there's something we missed," Skid said, keeping an eye on Mrs. Otto's whereabouts.

"Maybe it's not metal," said Robbie, with a look of disappointment. "Remember from ancient history: battle gear sometimes was made from leather or wood. It wouldn't set off a metal detector."

We all sighed.

Skid suggested, "Before we do any more digging, let's give Dr. Stallard a look at the belt."

"Yeah," Robbie said, and closed the book.

"Wait, wait!" I cried. "Who owns Telanoo? I have to know!"

"Shhh!" Mrs. Otto came tromping over. "Are you kids finished with that book?" She reached for it. "It's time."

I wanted to say that I'd quit talking if she'd quit tromping, but she would have tossed us out for sure. I'd been needing this information forever. "I'm sorry, Mrs. Otto," I said. "We have to find one more thing. Just one more minute. Please." I was glad to grovel.

"One minute!" she announced to the world.

"Hurry," I told Robbie. He riffled through the book until he came to page 21 again and found a tiny paragraph in the corner of Telanoo. "Here it is, here it is!" He read: "Alfred Theobald to—"

His head popped up. He looked creeped out. "It's been blotted out! The name's been blotted out!"

We were all in deep thought while Mrs. Otto—with a lemur scowl of disapproval—made a copy of the map.

Chapter 4

※※※

SNOW came down heavy on our way back to The Castle. We talked about where to meet with Dr. Stallard to show him the belt. I had my reservations about his coming, but everyone else seemed to think it was a good idea.

The attic of The Castle was a weird place to take a big-city scientist. Camp was out: too busy. The coffee shop was out: everyone's a regular customer. Dr. Stallard would stick out like a sore thumb, and we needed to keep a low profile.

"Oh no, I just thought of something," I said to Skid. "What about your parents? Won't Dr. Stallard tell them he's coming?"

Skid said, "Don't panic, Creek. I handled it before. I can handle it now."

That's all he was going to say.

"I'd like details," I said. As the leader of the group, it was my right.

He stopped dead, shoved his hands in his pockets and faced me, nose to nose, with huge flakes of snow falling between us. "Here it is, all laid out," he said. "Dad and I went up to Chicago last month. I asked Dad if we could see Dr. Stallard, that I was getting interested in archaeology. We tracked him down to a museum. I asked for a tour. Stallard obliged. When I got him alone, I slipped him the piece of chain mail and said

I'd be in touch. Couple days later he called, asked where we got it; I said the other pieces were in good hands. Later he wrote us about the gold links in the chain mail. The end. You got a problem with that?"

"Just make sure to check with me—with the group—first."

He saluted casually. "Yes, sir. Am I court-martialed, sir?"

I shot a glance at Reece. She was watching me, not him.

"At ease, Private," I said, smiling.

Skid said, "What do you say I send Mei's sketches to Dr. Stallard, as a preview for our top secret meeting? But only on your orders, sir!"

I looked at the others. "What do you think?"

Mei said, "That is a good idea."

Robbie and Reece agreed.

While Aunt Grace pulled the car around to take us all home, we waited in the front hall.

"We have to decide fast," I said. "Where should we meet?"

Mei said, "We can come to my house!"

"Good idea," Reece said.

We guys were leery. Mei was so quiet, we didn't know much about her or her family. Could they be trusted?

"Not sure . . ." I said.

Mei piled up reasons. "My mother would like visitors, and to meet my friends. My brother and sister are in college, and she is lonely. My father works very late every night. He will not be there. It will be private."

"How will we explain the meeting?" I asked.

"The truth, . . ." Reece said in a preachy tone, "that a professor is here to talk to Mei and her friends about local archaeology."

"My mother can make dinner for us. She will enjoy it." Mei gave us a pleading look. "I will be so happy to help my friends."

We guys still doubted this was the best idea, but no one wanted to tell her no and make her cry.

Reece looked at me. "*Daijoubu?*"

How could I say no? "That settles it. *Daijoubu.*"

A few days later, Skid was waiting at my locker. "Dr. Stallard called the minute he got the sketches. He wants to meet with us tomorrow."

When Mei got the news her mouth dropped open. "My mother must shop *today!*"

Mei lived on a nice street in a plain, one-story brick house. She didn't warn us ahead of time that we'd have to take off our shoes at the door. I yanked mine off and grimaced. Hanging off my feet were the gray, holey remains of last Christmas's traditional big bag o' socks. Pathetic. Mei offered me slippers, but my heels hung over the backs and looked goofy.

She'd already described her house, I guess so we wouldn't make jokes about it. "My parents didn't buy too much furniture. We are in America for two years. And Japan is very crowded, so we like a big empty house."

She showed us around. Her room was purple and pink with just a bed and a desk. The other bedrooms were bare and plain too, with only a bed and dresser each. The den was empty except for a table holding a fancy Japanese box about two feet square. It was dark wood with gold-trimmed doors open on the front. Inside sat a black-and-white picture of an old Japanese woman. The picture was surrounded by candlesticks, flowers, and signs in Japanese.

"That's Mei's grandmother," Reece said.

"This is where we pray," said Mei.

"You pray to your grandmother?" I asked.

Mei nodded. "It's our tradition."

I thought Reece would get on her case, like she does me when I say something about religion she doesn't like. She and Skid exchanged secret looks. Then she said, "Mei misses her grandma. I think they have the same smile, don't you?"

The doorbell rang at the stroke of 5:00.

Dr. Stallard, as it turned out, was two people.

A skinny couple showed up wearing khaki outfits and hiking boots—like they were heading out on safari. They introduced themselves as Dr. Eloise and Dr. Dale, doctors of science. They were gaunt like Mr. Dowland, but energetic and talkative with bright eyes and pink cheeks. They looked sixty maybe but acted much younger. He carried a battered briefcase. She had a camera.

Mei let them in and showed them to the bathroom where

they could freshen up. Skid leaned over at me in the hallway and said between his teeth. "I didn't know she was coming, I swear!"

My eyebrows went up, resigned. "Too late now. We have to go with it."

"I've met her only once before. I didn't know she was a scientist too. I didn't invite her."

"Forget it." I should have been miffed, this being top-secret business, but Skid was feeling bad enough. I asked, "You told them we don't have the helmet and arm piece anymore, didn't you? That we just have the belt?"

"Was I supposed to?"

My heart sank. "Well, yeah!"

"Listen," he said, "I sent the sketches like you said. He called to set up a time. That's it."

"You should have told them!"

He glared at me. "I didn't have high-level clearance."

Mrs. Aizawa, Mei's mom, bowed and waved everyone into the dining room and served tea. Reece and Robbie were good at chitchat, so I let them have at it. I kept thinking about that bombshell I had to drop: the Stallard's had come all this way to see two pieces of God's armor, and I'd lost them—a big deal any way you slice it.

The first course was soup: a little boiled quail egg and a couple of weeds swimming around by themselves in broth. Then the main course: steak and vegetables and rice, which was really good. Mei showed us how to use chopsticks. Reece and Skid already knew how, Reece being Mei's best friend, and Skid being an army brat from all over the world. Robbie and I did pretty well, though I'll always think a spoon and fork make better sense. It was as good as a fancy restaurant, with lots of dishes and the best service.

Nothing was said about the armor while we ate. Instead the Stallards talked a lot about the history of the Hopewell and Adena Indians, ancient mounds in the area and things like that, for the benefit of Mrs. Aizawa. We were saving the important stuff for the private meeting.

After the meal Mei's mom led us to a living room that had just a couch and a coffee table, a lamp, a bookcase, and a stack of cushions to sit on. She bowed and backed out of the room. The scientists and Reece sat on the couch; the rest of us sat around the coffee table on cushions. Skid got his coat from the closet and joined us. He broke the news to the Stallards. I appreciated how he did it, not mentioning me by name.

"We have good news and we have bad news," he said, laying his coat on the coffee table. He unfolded it carefully, saying, "The bad news is that the helmet and arm piece have been stolen from us by the man who buried them in the first place." Before the Stallards could react, he said, "But I sent you the sketches Mei made, so you know what they look like. And the good news is—"

Mei handed plastic gloves to Skid. He put them on quickly and unveiled the belt, spreading it out on the coffee table.

The Stallards moved like they were surgically joined at the shoulder, leaning way over until their chins almost touched their knees. They made mouth noises and muttered to each other, phrases like "interesting workmanship" and about "confounding certain skeptics," at which point they chuckled low. They commented on the condition of the leather and judged it fair and relatively new. They bickered some over whether the leather was original, and what might be considered "original."

"Debatable," Dr. Dale said. He adjusted his bifocals to examine different parts of the belt, finally fixing his eyes on the buckle. "Ah, there it is, yes, Eloise. Hebrew is it not? Primitive, but there. Do you see it?"

"Yes, yes . . . " she nodded. Closing her eyes, she whispered, "It is the omen belt."

"Omen?" I asked.

Her eyes popped open and jumped to my face. "The Ancient Omen!" she chirped, with a strangely excited smile. Her gray eyes sparkled.

I don't mind saying I was a little uneasy about all these eyes glittering around me in recent days—first Reece and Skid, now the two Dr. Stallards.

People often remind me of animals, like I said. Mrs. Stallard looked at that moment like a wild turkey, skinny neck and jerky head, in a nervous thrill over her pile of corn.

After some time the Stallards sat up and gave each other a high five, which seemed pretty silly to me: two high-fiving senior citizens on safari in a bare Japanese living room, all over a dirty belt. It was weird. Not freak-show weird, but not your typical evening either. And besides that, I wondered why they were smiling. I'd always thought an omen was *bad* news.

Chapter 5

THE Stallards said they would need to take the belt back to Chicago for scientific tests. They promised to keep everything under wraps. I was about to get bummed out about letting another piece of the armor out of my sight, but since I was the one to lose the other pieces in the first place, I had no room to talk. Skid trusted them; Reece did too, which meant Mei probably did, and Robbie too, I guess.

We told them everything we knew: that Stanford Dowland was a preacher who brought the armor over from a castle in Ireland; that after he preached some sermons on it, his little congregation fell apart and closed down; that he buried the armor, but when we found it, he dug it up and buried it someplace else.

"What about the possibility of meeting Mr. Dowland? Could such a thing be arranged, I wonder?" Dr. Eloise asked.

I told them how determined he was to keep the armor a secret, how strange he'd acted, and how his vicious dog had come after us.

Robbie added, "And it would have killed us if Elijah hadn't shot it with arrows and if Skid hadn't hacked it to death with a shovel!"

They got quiet and blinked at each other. Dr. Dale said,

"For now we should pursue every other option without involving adults."

We agreed.

The coolest thing was what they had discovered about the little piece of chain mail. Dr. Dale opened his raggedy briefcase and brought it out, unwrapping it very carefully from the old rag. He placed it in his wife's hand. I felt silly being so excited about a scrap of mesh wrapped in a rag, but there you have it. "The mail is very, very fine," said Dr. Stallard. He went into lecture mode, but it wasn't boring. "Historically armor was used for battle and for ceremonies, as in royal processions. These links are so very fine, most assuredly the piece this came from was not used in a real battle."

We guys were naturally disappointed to get the official word, but not Reece. "You mean a *military* battle," she corrected. "There are many kinds of battles."

"Yes, of course," he said, looking at her curiously. "But here's the surprising discovery I wrote you about. See these links right here? See how they are a different color?"

We closed in around Dr. Eloise's hand.

"They are gold," said Mei.

"Pure gold," she corrected.

"But not a treasure?" Robbie asked, disappointed.

"Hardly," she answered. "A mere fragment. But very interesting, especially what is engraved on it."

"Engraved?" Reece gasped.

"You gotta be kidding!" I said.

Robbie said, "No way! Where?"

Dr. Dale pulled a little velvet bag out of his pocket and emptied into his hand a lens mounted in black metal, about an inch and a half square.

"This is a linen tester," he said. "It's used to count the number of threads in fabric for quality control. Not as good as a microscope, of course, but much more portable. And," he laughed, "I dare not bring anything of value on long trips. I tend to lose things. Sadly, all that rot about absent-minded professors is true."

I was already worrying that he'd lose God's belt on the way back to Chicago, when his wife giggled, "Once he left a piece of Etruscan pottery in a hotel room. I was livid, as you might imagine. But since I had once lost our daughter at Tel el-Amarna, and got halfway to Cairo before realizing it, I had no room to talk!"

"You lost . . . your daughter?" Reece asked.

"Just once or twice," she said with a wave of her hand.

"Wasn't she scared?" Mei asked.

"Heavens no! She was ten years old, perfectly capable, knew a bit of the language. A nice family took her in. She watered camels and played video games—had the time of her life. She was fine . . . on *that* trip anyway."

Dr. Dale said, "I suppose we think differently about children than most people do. We don't worry."

All of a sudden those two senior safari scientists seemed pretty cool.

"Here! Have a look," Dr. Eloise said. "Let's move under the lamp for the best light." She unfolded the linen tester and offered it to me. "Now look for the gold links. It will take some wiggling of those little rascals to see the engraving."

I wiggled those little rascals for a good minute. Finally I found numbers etched into each gold ring. "I see it! It says . . . 22 . . . and . . . 25." I looked up confused. "22, 25? What's that mean?"

"You see? Isn't this such a fascinating mystery!" Dr. Eloise said happily, and I could hardly wait for her answer. "On modern jewelry the weight of the gold is stamped somewhere, on the back of the piece or perhaps the clasp. It might say 10 carat or 14 carat. That was our first idea about the meaning of the numbers. But pure gold—with no alloys added—is 24 carat, not more. So that can't be it!"

Either this lady was a glutton for bad news or she had something up her sleeve.

"So . . . what is it?" Reece asked.

"We don't know!" she chirped. "But we have ingested untold gallons of hot tea day and night to get to the bottom of it!"

Her glazed eyes made sense now: caffeine rush.

Dr. Dale took over. "In ancient times gold was not just a precious metal; some believed it had magical powers. An armorer might put a few links of gold into a weapon or armor piece, to insure good luck on the battlefield. But the fine quality of these links suggests that the armor was used for ceremony. Do the gold links make a kind of decorative design, we asked ourselves? Are the numbers a mark to identify the soldier it was issued to?"

"Both!" Robbie made a stab at it.

"Neither!" I tried.

"Both of you might be right," Dr. Eloise said. "Except, . . . " she said cryptically, "except for this . . . "

I wiped sweat from my forehead. She was wearing me out with suspense.

She curled her finger at her husband. He handed over the sketches of the arm piece from his briefcase. "Except for this," she said again, pointing to the engraved *koinonia*.

Robbie said, "We've *seen* that already." His patience was wearing thin.

"What armorer would engrave the word *fellowship* on battle armor, or even on ceremonial armor?" she asked. "Wouldn't he engrave *victory?* Or the name of the king? But *fellowship?* Ridiiiiculous!"

She was going to string us along into the next decade.

"22, 25?" Mei said thoughtfully.

"Do you have *any* leads?" I asked the Stallards.

"Could it be a numerical code for another Bible word?" Skid asked.

Dr. Eloise bubbled over. "Brilliant, Marcus! Children, I believe Marcus is correct in his deduction!"

Robbie asked, "Deduction? What deduction?"

Ignoring him she opened her hand, palm up. Dr. Dale

pulled a Bible out of his briefcase and put it in her hand like he was giving her a surgical tool. She held it out to us dramatically, "The Book is a living thing, children, a living thing. I anticipate the wonderful messages we'll find."

I slumped. "Okay, I'm totally lost."

Reece was smiling, like it was all clear as a bell to her.

Dr. Dale chimed in. "Who knows what secrets we will discover . . . that is, *if* all the pieces can be retrieved!"

"Yeah," Robbie sneered at me, "if *Elijah* can keep from losing them."

I wanted to strangle him. The professors shot me a look. My face turned hot. They turned away quickly, acting as if they hadn't heard what Robbie said. Everyone stood in that bare room looking around for something to stare at instead of me, the irresponsible chowderhead.

Then Reece looked at me with pure happiness. "What's over is over. Elijah found the pieces in the first place, and he'll find them again!"

"To the task!" said Dr. Dale.

"Precisely," said his wife.

"The plot thickens," piped in Robbie dramatically.

"Ready, aim, fire," said the army brat, Skid.

"*Ganbatte!*" chimed in Mei.

"Yeah," was all I could think to say.

We showed them the glued compass, explained how it pointed back to the old ruin of a house, and that we were going back there to see what we could find.

Before they left, the Stallards made us get in a circle and hold hands. They asked if anyone wanted to pray. Right away, Reece said, "Yes, please." I bowed my head and closed my eyes like I'd seen people do. Once I peeked at Reece. Her face was raised to the ceiling. She went on about how wonderful and great God was. She thanked him for the quest and the Stallards and each one of us by name—which felt awkward, but good. She even prayed for Mr. Dowland, that whatever happened to him years ago might be put to rest. Finally she asked if she could please have the strength to go into Telanoo with the rest of us for the next part of the search—but that if she couldn't, that was okay. She ended with, "Your will be done."

Let her go, I thought to myself. *Please let her go with us.* A feeling of peace washed over me.

How could I know that the next leg of our search would lead us into things we didn't *want* to know, throwing the whole town of Magdeline into chaos and anger, with all fingers pointing at me.

Chapter 6

✖✖✖

AFTER the Stallards left, I suggested we keep searching land plat records in the courthouse or wherever for the owner of Telanoo. Reece and Skid thought that snooping through court files would arouse suspicion. "Okay then," I said, "I'll go to a real estate office and pretend I'm on an errand from my dad."

Reece rolled her eyes and said it would get back to him for sure.

I skulked out to the hallway to put my shoes back on. *I don't know what's up with her sometimes*, I thought. *They were good ideas and they might have worked.*

Reece was always telling me I should go to church. For some odd reason, the recent experience in the rat-infested emptiness of Old Pilgrim Church had left me curious. But I agreed to go to the community Thanksgiving service with her mostly because she said the minister was going to preach about the Indians. To tell the truth, it was also because if I said no, it would be just Skid and her there together. Robbie and Mei would be out of town.

Skid still liked Miranda Varner, or so he said. But he hadn't worked up the nerve to ask her out, which kept me on edge about him and Reece. I couldn't figure why someone who'd been all over the world, and who was so cool that the rest of us were gutter slush by comparison . . . I didn't get why he was so shy.

Reece's church was fifteen miles west of Magdeline, on a smooth ridge of grass with a basketball court at one end of the parking lot. It was big and bright outside and in. There were some pretty amazing windows with stained glass scenes of Jesus sitting on a rock talking to people, Jesus praying on a rock, and Jesus standing in front of a rock with his arms out and a glow all around him. With all those rocks around, it looked like he lived in Telanoo. I pointed this out to Reece and joked: "I hope that isn't the same rock in all three windows, because that would mean he was stuck in the same spot forever, just talking, praying, and glowing."

She jabbed me in the ribs and told me to shut up. I said, "You shouldn't say 'shut up' in church."

"*You* just did," she snipped back.

There was another window of Jesus out in a field with sheep, which was nice.

The place was packed with chattering people. Then the music started. Without Skid on one side and Reece on the other, I'd have felt supremely dumb. It's hard to explain why. I figured there were rules to follow, but nobody told me what they were.

If I got bored, I was going to imagine myself at an awards show, with my bodyguard and press agent at my sides. I'd be called up to that impressive stage to say something, and everyone would cheer.

(Before you criticize me for mentally drifting off in church, remember that I didn't know the songs. Even if I did, I can't carry a tune in a bucket. And I'm a man of action more than a man of words.)

Just like Reece said, the minister had dug up stuff about what Native Americans believed. He said many worshiped the creator and called him the One Above. He read Bible ideas that matched what the Indians believed. I agreed with a lot of it. The minister said that silence is sometimes the voice of the One Above, and that we should be silent often to hear the creator's voice. Then he read: "Be still, and know that I am God."

"That sounds like your vision quest," Reece whispered.

"Yeah," I whispered. I drifted back to that night again, when it felt like my whole universe went silent. The memory of it hadn't dimmed at all but had gotten stronger every time I recalled it.

The preacher said that the One Above had many names in Indian thought: Master of Breath, Creator, Moneto, God, and Ruler of All That Is, Was, or Ever Can Be. Then he spewed a whole list of names from the Bible, like light and vine and Redeemer. He ended with Jesus.

I had figured out a long time ago that Jesus was a great teacher, but no one ever had told me Jesus was the same as God. It was kind of a jolt. My eyes settled on the stained glass Jesus, glowing in front of the rock, as the preacher talked on about the Indian ideas. The creator doesn't spoil the created with too many gifts or easy answers, he said, but that everything, even every struggle, has purpose. And we should seek our purpose and give thanks for it.

The preacher ended by telling the whole crowd we should be thankful for a country that was not originally ours, but which we were blessed to live in. And to ask forgiveness for how our forefathers and their native brothers cruelly mistreated each other, and may it never happen again, and so on and so on. He ended with a prayer.

If Indians get talked about every week, I thought, *I might not mind church.*

A big song from the organ blasted everyone to the back of the church and out into the cold.

Grandma wasn't coming up until Christmas, so my family had Thanksgiving dinner by ourselves. I spent the afternoon in my room, digesting turkey and studying the map we'd copied from the library book. The ruin wasn't too far from the west end of Council Cliffs State Park, which gave me a new angle on getting there without having to go through Telanoo. Getting someone to drop us off in the park would save a lot of legwork. Problem was, the map didn't show what kind of terrain lay between the park and the ruin. *Probably no worse than Telanoo.* It would make no difference to me, being an outdoorsman. But I had to think about Reece.

I sat on my bed, propped against the log wall, planning our next move. . . .

Next to Owl Woods, my room was my favorite place. When we moved here six years ago, my room was crawling with stenciled bears and puppies. Aunt Grace wanted to help me with decorating, but I begged Mom in private not to let her force her frills on me. Mom said I could have a guy-type room if, and only if (this was blackmail pure and simple), I kept it clean. Otherwise, Aunt Grace would have free reign.

My bed sat against the log wall, under the window where I could see the sky as I fell asleep. My bow and arrows hung on the opposite wall next to a genuine Indian rug Mom and Dad bought me in Gatlinburg. I had started an arrowhead collection, which was on a shelf, but I only had five so far. My room was the smallest because the twins needed lots of toy space. I didn't mind; I spent more time outdoors than in.

From my second-floor window I could see our backyard, the side of the lodge, and the camp pool. While I sat staring at the burned and blackened hole that once was Old Pilgrim Church, the phone rang. It was Reece. She sounded excited and upset.

"My dad's in town," she said. "He just popped in. He'll be here for only a couple of days. So if you were going back to the ruin . . ."

"We'll wait," I said.

Long pause. "I don't think you should."

"A couple of days won't matter."

"It could matter. The temperature's dropping every day.

If the ground freezes, you can't dig. You guys should go on. Mei's still out of town."

"But you prayed to go," I said.

"And the answer I'm hearing is no." She didn't sound disappointed.

"If you're sure."

"Positive. Just be very, very careful."

Hesitantly, I told her about the possibility of getting to the ruin through the park, that I didn't know how rough a hike it would be.

"See? It all works out. That settles it."

The hint of relief in her voice told me how hard the last hike through Telanoo had been.

We hung on the line a minute, saying nothing.

"Have a nice time with your dad," I said.

"Thanks. Did you like the church service?"

"Yeah."

"I hoped you would."

"I didn't like the organ music though."

"That's okay. Well, you be careful. Take your bow and arrows."

"Dowland doesn't have any more demon dogs," I joked.

She laughed, and said in a sinister way, "Not that we know of."

"Oh, thanks. I feel better now."

"The walkie-talkies don't reach that far, huh?"

"Not from camp. We'll be on our own."

Out of the blue, I remembered the old movie *Gorgo* and a scene when people capture this giant flesh-eating reptile that's terrorizing the coast. They think all their troubles are over, that they have this great scientific find. What they don't know is that he's the baby. When their backs are turned, up pops the parent out of a crack in the ocean floor and swallows them whole.

But that was science fiction.

Chapter 7

NONE of the moms would have dropped us off in Council Cliffs without asking questions. Could you imagine me saying, "Hey, Mom, how about putting me out in a state park in the dead of winter, and don't come back?"

Yeah, that'd go over big.

Robbie was due back in the morning, and Skid was free all weekend. I called Justin Brill, because his big brother Jeremy had his own car and could probably be bought off cheap. Eighteen years old and two sizes bigger than his kid brother, Jeremy got on the phone and said he'd drive us for a few bucks. I set up a time and place.

"It'll be one way, Jeremy," I made clear. "You won't have to hang around or come back and pick us up."

"Fine by me. You going hunting, Nature Boy?"

"Yeah. Hunting."

The day was calm, with a few big puffy clouds. I wore a tan jacket and jeans to blend in with the landscape. Skid showed up in his usual head-to-toe black. Robbie wore a bright red jacket so he wouldn't be shot by hunters.

"It's bow season for deer hunting," I explained. "Half the time we'll be in the park where hunting's not allowed. Don't go paranoid on us."

We took the usual gear: canteen, knife, bandanna, snacks, binoculars; and what we needed for the search: map, metal detector, shovel, my bow with hundred grain broadhead arrows—big enough to bring down a bear—and a real working compass. I hardly ever used a compass, but we needed precision here.

Following the winding road through the park, we pointed Jeremy Brill to the spot nearest Telanoo and had him drop us off. We started unloading our equipment.

"Hey, jerks, how about my money?"

"Give us a minute!" I said.

He eyed our gear. "What are you guys up to with that shovel, anyhow?" he asked.

"Exploring," I answered, and slammed the car door.

He rolled down his window. "Exploring what? I thought you were hunting."

We looked at each other. I was ready to blurt out the truth like Reece always did, that we were looking for an ancient treasure. Skid beat me to it in his own way. He sauntered around to Jeremy's window, tossed in a couple of bills, and said, "None of your business, Brill."

Jeremy snorted, "Well, good luck, you kiddies. Hope you don't get lost and start crying for your mommies to come find you." He tore out and was gone.

I thought for sure Skid would be miffed. He just laughed and gave us a mission-accomplished nod.

We set off due west. The woods were old and tall and scraggly, the undergrowth dense. We kept a straight course into the cold wind, except when we had to swing around big, tall clumps of brambles. I had an uneasy feeling heading toward Telanoo. That place always rattled me.

Huffing and puffing, Robbie said, "I don't know what more we can find at the ruin."

"We missed something important," I said, plowing ahead. "The compass pointed there. The next piece of armor has to be there."

"Maybe not," Robbie pouted. "I did a good job before with the metal detector."

"I know, but we have to look again," I replied. "I didn't mean anything by it. Don't be so touchy."

"I'm not!" Robbie barked.

"Maybe Dowland hasn't buried anything there *yet*," Skid threw out his idea.

I stopped. "You think we jumped the gun on him?" I hadn't thought of that.

Robbie stopped too. "Maybe we shouldn't go. What if he's there burying it right now? What if he sees us coming?"

The last thing I wanted was another face-to-face with Stan Dowland.

Skid spoke up: "I say we go, but carefully; and look ahead. Don't leave tracks. Wherever we dig, we cover it over."

"Oh, pickle!" said Robbie. "You know what just hit me again? Ancient history."

"You're weird," I said.

"I mean what I said at the library before, that some ancient battle gear had no metal. Shoes might be all leather, a shield might be wood overlaid with leather."

"*Could* be metal," Skid said optimistically.

"Or not," Robbie went on. "How will we find—"

"Fresh dirt," I said and started walking again. "We'll spot it. I'm good at this kind of thing." It was cold, but I'd worked up a sweat; and Robbie's doubts were working on me. *It could be a dead end.* "I've said this before, but I don't think Dowland could make it to the ruin, even this way. He's so old and frail."

"Someone buried something there," Skid said. "The compass says so."

"What if he has an accomplice?" was Robbie's next theory.

I hadn't thought of that either.

Skid sneered, "Don't make it worse than it is, kid."

"Don't call me kid. I'm older than you."

"You don't look it."

"I'm ignoring that." Robbie stopped for a drink from the canteen. "Remember the old man said, 'Piece by piece they will rest in peace. Like the ones in the ground.' If the ground's frozen, we might have to wait until spring."

Doubts or not, I wasn't about to have the search derailed. I wanted to find the full armor and put it on, like I'd been told by . . . by God. Or whoever. "We're talking in circles. I say we shut up and keep our eyes and ears open."

"When we get there, let's treat it like a crime scene," Skid suggested. "Measure it off into a grid and search square by square."

We came out of the woods of Council Cliffs State Park onto a wide meadow with tall grass the color of my jacket. The long, flat field was surrounded by the hills of the park wrapping around behind us, the rolling ridges of Ohio farm country to our right, and the strange cliff ahead that we called Devil's Cranium. We plowed on across the field.

"There!" said Robbie. "There it is!"

We were a few hundred yards off course to the north. We'd overshot our mark, but not by much. The ruin stood just as we'd left it—a crumbling stone chimney and the last remains of a house hunkered down in a thicket.

We kept low, watching and listening for signs of life. There was nothing alive in that pale field but us. We moved with stealth, circling wide around the ruin to make sure the coast was clear. Hooking up with the path we'd made before, we traced along the very route where vicious Salem had pursued us in dead earnest.

We smelled him before we saw him.

"Peeeyoooo!" Robbie said.

The elements already had been working on the big black malamute's carcass. His eyes were dried and sunk in, his shriveled mouth frozen in a snarl and crawling with bugs. My arrows were still sticking out of him.

We pulled the necks of our shirts up over our noses. Robbie

turned to Skid. "Garoosss! Leave no footprints, you said? We left a lot more than footprints!"

Skid said to me, "Yank out those arrows, Elijah. They're a dead giveaway as to how he died."

I sucked in air, yanked one out, backed away, and dragged it through the grass to wipe off the decay. I went back for the second one but couldn't do it. I needed fresh air.

"What if Dowland's already seen this?" Robbie asked.

"He hasn't," I tried to sound confident. "There's no easy way to get here. I'm telling you he couldn't make it."

"He stalked you all night, remember?" Robbie said. "He could be on his way right now."

Skid snapped, "You're a bundle of optimism, Wingate." He turned to me. "We won't be able to stand it, working here with that stench. We have to bury him." He nodded to the right. "I'll dig a hole over there in the bushes, way past the house. We'll drop Salem in and cover him over good."

I probably could've handled the smell a little better than the other guys. I'd cleaned out a boa constrictor cage at the nature center, after it . . . you know. That stink will bring tears to your eyes. But rotting malamute was no bouquet of flowers either. I was grateful for Skid's offer.

"Thanks," I said and grabbed the sleeve of Robbie's jacket. "Let's start on the other side of the ruin. We'll make long straight passes, like mowing the yard. Side by side, so we don't miss anything."

Robbie and I dug our toes here and there looking for soft

spots. In the back of my mind, I kept stewing over what Dowland would do when he discovered I'd killed his precious Salem. As if he weren't already mad enough at me for breaking into his garage and refusing to give up on the search for the armor. Not to mention I'd threatened to tell all his neighbors if he didn't spill the story behind Old Pilgrim Church. He had a bucket load of reasons not to like me.

"Find a place to bury that dog yet?" I called to Skid after a few minutes.

"I'm looking, I'm looking," he called back, heading farther into the weeds.

It was a dry, desolate feeling, the lonely sounds of our feet crunching hard ground, Skid's shovel testing the rocky soil: *tch, tch . . . tch . . . tch.*

No wonder this farm failed, I said to myself. *They probably starved to death.*

"The treasure can't be here, the ground's too hard," Robbie said.

"It has to be here," I insisted.

"Maybe it's farther back toward the park," he said. "Or *in* the park."

I scanned the place we'd come from: Council Cliffs State Park, a thousand acres of woods and cliffs, caves and waterfalls.

Robbie followed my gaze. "Dowland could get there easy, Elijah. All he'd have to do is drive in after dark and find a spot where there are no trails or picnic areas."

I didn't want to buy the idea, mostly because of the

hopeless, sinking feeling it gave me. We could spend years searching the park and never find a thing.

Skid was still milling around on the other side of the ruin, poking here and there with the point of his shovel.

"Hurry it up, Skid; we're dying from the smell over here."

I turned back to Robbie. He was starting to work the metal detector, muttering about a needle in a haystack.

"Keep going," I said.

"I went over this area last time," he complained. "There's nothing—"

The sound of splintering wood came from Skid's direction. I heard him yell. When I looked up he was gone.

Robbie dropped his metal detector. "What happened? What was that?"

"Skid!" I hightailed it over fallen stone and brambles toward where I'd seen him last. "Skid!" I tore across the field, hearing nothing, seeing nobody. Robbie cried out something from where he was. "Stay there!" I yelled back at him.

I heard a groan and followed it through the high dead grass. What I saw threw me back in shock.

There was Skid, flat on his back, grimacing in pain, and missing a leg from the knee down.

Chapter 8

"I'M okay," he said. "I stepped on a board and it fell through. There's a hole under here."

I breathed a huge sigh of relief. But when he tried to sit up, the wood beneath him cracked and sagged. Fear shot through me. "Don't move!" I yelled. "You're sitting on rotten wood!"

I ran around by his head, testing every dry, grassy step. Quick but careful, I scooped my arms under his armpits, in case the wood should let go.

He tried to raise his leg out, but something caught it. Blood seeped through his black jeans.

"Don't yank!" he yelled. "Something's got the back of my knee!"

I planted one knee on hard soil. "Stay calm, man. Hold on."

Robbie came running.

"Watch your step!" I warned him back. "Bring the canteen and the bandanna." I turned back to Skid. "I'm going to ease you this way. See if you can pull free from the broken end of that plank."

He worked himself out easy-does-it as I dragged him away from the hole. He had a long gash behind the knee. I flushed it with water and wrapped it with the bandanna. He winced and got to his feet. "Thanks. I'm good to go."

The three of us yanked the old boards off the hole, which was two-and-a-half feet across. We leaned over it.

"It's deep!" Robbie said.

"Looks like an abandoned well," I said.

Skid said, "Then I got a lucky break on the grave digging. Let's dump old Salem in that hole and get on with it."

Robbie leaned farther in. "I think it's dry."

"Careful," I said again. I looked at the sky. "Give that cloud a minute. When it passes, we should have some light down there."

Slowly the cloud passed. Sunlight beamed down on us and into the well. We peered in. There in a puddle of black water at the bottom were big splinters of rotted boards, some old rags . . . and what looked like a human skeleton.

Chapter 9

ROBBIE screamed and fell back. His hands flew to his face. "A body!"

The sun cast bright rays on the well's stone sides and lit the murky bottom. There was no mistake. They were most definitely human remains.

Skid's voice was flat and serious. "That's what it is. We have to tell the police."

Our heads met over the hole. We stared silently at the bones and a skull and what was left of the clothes.

The first thing out of my mouth was, "Dad will know I've been here."

"All our parents will know," said Skid, thinking on the same track. He glanced at me and said aloud what flashed into all our minds: "They'll know everything."

Everything. It didn't take long to sink in.

I said, "We'll have to tell them about the armor? about the Stallards?"

"Man," Skid said, shaking his head. "I never told my parents they were in town. The whole story will come out."

Robbie backed away from the hole, his hands still clamped over his face. In spite of our predicament, relief suddenly rushed over me. I was glad Reece and Mei hadn't come along. This was too gruesome for girls.

Anxiously I ran my hand through my hair, coaching myself to calm down, to stop and think. Skid shoved his hands into his pockets and kicked at the dirt.

"Dowland will know too!" Robbie suddenly burst out. "This will be in the papers, and he'll know we killed Salem!" He whirled to me. "He'll know how *you* killed him, Elijah, with your bow and arrows, and *you* with a shovel, Skid!"

"Salem attacked us, Robbie!" I yelled back. "It was self-defense. But thanks for sharing the blame!"

Skid seemed satisfied that his leg had stopped bleeding. "Stay cool, guys. We can't bow out now. This is a crime scene. We shouldn't touch anything else."

I stared off toward Devil's Cranium. *We're in deep as it is, out here with a shovel at the scene of a murder, and no good reason for it.*

The sun went behind a cloud, throwing the well and the ruin and the three of us into shadow. Then out it came again, back and forth, light and shadow, like a searchlight, and we were criminals caught in the act.

"You may need stitches," I said. "We should get going."

Skid didn't answer. Again and again our eyes were drawn down into the hole.

Robbie said: "We shouldn't have been here in the first place. We were trespassing."

"But no one owns it," I said. "The name was blotted off the map."

"Someone has to own it," Skid said, being logical, "even if he died. Even if that person in the well is the owner himself."

I started pacing, just to use up some adrenaline, thinking out loud, "This is where the compass pointed. Not to the next piece of armor, like we hoped, but to a body."

"My mom and dad will kill me!" Robbie said. "They think I'm at your house right now!"

"Okay, so we didn't tell the exact truth the whole time," I said. "We haven't done anything wrong. We found old relics, followed the clues, killed a dog who attacked us, and found a dead body. We're in the clear."

Skid sat and squeezed the pain out of his wound. "I don't know, man," he said doubtfully, "we're not really in the clear."

"Okay, then," I said, "we can explain about finding the armor in the basement of Old Pilgrim Church, and—"

"We can't!" Robbie came to his feet. "They'll think we set the fire and burned the church down! You saw how the firefighters looked at us that night. No one else was around. They already suspect us."

"No, they don't. It was ruled inconclusive," I said, "and besides, nobody cares. Everyone's glad to be rid of the old building."

"We're going to jail!" Robbie wailed.

"Dowland set the fire," I said firmly. "If anyone will get into trouble, it will be him. We know that."

Skid shook his head, got up, and strolled over to peer into the well again. "We *don't* know that. Actually, there's very little we do know about anything. We're in the dark, just like that poor guy down there."

Robbie said, "We don't have to tell them we were even in Old Pilgrim Church."

"Dad knows we were, remember?" I said. "I told him, at least the first time. But no one will make the connection between the old church and this. Will they?"

Robbie's quick brain drilled right through that idea. "Yes, they will! Because how else do we explain being here, unless we backtrack all the way to the armor which we discovered in the church, and dug up from the cemetery, and which was lost in Telanoo, which led us to the forked path, which led us to Devil's Cranium, where we dug up the compass, which led us here—to a body?"

Swirling through my mind came a dozen explanations I could offer to get us off the hook. I could say we were working on a school project, or that Jeremy Brill had known a body was out here and paid us money to find it. I could blame Skid, saying it was all his insane idea for a secret club, or that we'd followed Dowland here. Most of the explanations even made pretty good sense, but none was actually true. When I realized this, something rose up in my chest—a hard question that would nag at me for a long time: *how'd I get so good at lying?*

My stomach felt heavy. Suddenly Salem's stench filled my nose, even my mouth. Nausea rolled up into my throat. I swallowed in disgust. Looking in the hole made me dizzy. I felt as if I were falling in. I reeled back to save myself the same fate as that guy.

"The police will ask us why we were digging here," Skid

said rather calmly, as if from far away. "They'll want to know what we were looking for."

"We could just leave," Robbie answered, in a panic. "Not say a word. Forget the treasure hunt, forget Salem. Everything! Just go back to being our normal, innocent selves!"

While I forced myself to get a grip, Skid went on, thinking in a straight line, "Someone will find it, eventually . . . Jeremy Brill knows we were here; he brought us. They will ask us why we had a shovel out here at the scene of a murder . . . Guys, this looks really, really bad."

I braced myself for one last glance into the well, just to prove to myself that I could. The lonely white skull lay facedown at an angle, strangely calm, as if he'd nodded off to sleep. "Maybe it was an accident," I said weakly.

"Maybe," said Skid, but his gloomy voice said otherwise.

I said, "Let's get our things together, and take care where you step, just in case."

Robbie said, "I've got to get out of here. I'm going to throw up!" He grabbed his stuff and headed across the meadow toward Devil's Cranium. Skid and I stood there just looking at each other.

"Got any brilliant ideas?" he asked me dryly.

The cool Marcus Skidmore is asking my advice, looking to me for answers. What should we do?

Reece's voice floated into my ear. With knots of dread and determination in my throat, I said, "Here's what we do: we tell the truth. The whole truth."

Chapter 10

I couldn't find Dad.

Safely through Telanoo and back at camp, I sent Robbie and Skid home. No reason they should take the heat from my parents.

Dad wasn't at the house, in his office, or in the maintenance building. I checked the dining hall. The Mad River Boys had arrived, a different brood than last year, but still sour-faced and smelling like tobacco. They were finishing a meal. I walked past without making eye contact. Bo was organizing their next project with the counselors. I caught his eye and mouthed the words, "Where's Dad?" He pointed toward the Tree House Village.

Two men hammered away at big panels of drywall. I breathed in the welcome smell of new wood and tried to look calm. When I saw him in the central meeting room overseeing the construction, I became a bundle of nerves.

"Hey, Dad."

He was checking blueprints and glanced up. When he caught the look on my face—try as I did to be casual—his face went slack.

"Elijah, what's wrong?"

"I have to talk to you."

"Sure, what is it? Are you sick?"

"No, I . . . have to talk to you, in private."

"Give me just a minute." He went over to the men and said he'd be back in a few. He came back to me. "Okay. Let's go to my office."

I'd planned to start from the beginning, but once he sat down behind his desk, I sort of exploded, "We found a dead body."

He pitched forward in his chair. "A what?"

"A body."

"Where?"

"In a well."

"What well?"

"At some old farm."

"What old farm? Talk to me, son!"

I pointed northeast. "That way. Out behind the camp."

"What were you doing off the grounds, Elijah?"

I didn't answer.

Slowly he stood. "Did Mom know where you were?"

"No." I sort of crumpled in the chair in front of his desk. "I'm sorry, Dad, I'm sorry!"

He came around and squeezed my shoulder, patted me on the back, and talked soft: "It's okay, son. Just tell me. Start at the beginning."

"I can't start at the beginning. Can I start in the middle?"

"Start anywhere, Elijah, just tell me what you found . . . you're sure it was a *body*?"

I nodded. "A skeleton. At the bottom of a well, Dad. We

weren't trespassing. We went to the library to see who owned the land, and no one did, there was no name! It was blotted out!"

"He pulled up a chair and sat facing me. "Okay, slow down and make sense. Where?"

"This old farm, between here and Council Cliffs."

"What were you doing there in the first place? How did you get there?"

"We got a ride."

"You . . . sneaked away, without telling us?"

He read guilt all over my face. His forehead wrinkled. In the silence that followed, he was thinking back over the past months. "You've been acting different lately . . . those secret campfires, having those girls over . . . Elijah, what are you hiding?"

I couldn't answer. Suddenly my whole life flashed before me like they say happens right before you die. I saw all the sneaky things I'd done the last few months: lying about what we'd found in the church; lying that I knew nothing about the grave robbers; sneaking off to Newpoint without permission; lying to Mom and Robbie so I could go on my vision quest; the dozen other times I would have lied, only Reece stopped me.

And why did I have to lie? I asked myself? *Didn't Mom and Dad trust me, give me free reign? Didn't they count on me—with baby-sitting Nori and Stacy, with setting up campfires and finding little campers who wander off—because I'm the best fire maker, the best tracker? And couldn't I get free snacks and the golf cart anytime I wanted? Didn't everyone at school think I'm the luckiest dog because I live at Camp Mudj?*

From the beginning I wanted no adults in on our search for the armor of God, but why? I'd wanted it all for myself. I'd been a jerk to Reece a few weeks before. Now I was about to be a humongous disappointment to my dad.

For all my telling myself I'd been straight up about the quest, I had lied and lied and lied.

I looked into Dad's hurt eyes. He seemed to see right into my mind. "Elijah, what's going on here?"

"Nothing." I couldn't help lying just one more time—and hated myself as soon as I said it. He saw right through me.

He reached for the phone. "I have to call the police, Elijah. Do you know how to get back to the place where you found this . . . body?" He punched numbers.

"Yeah."

"Officer Taylor, please." He covered the mouthpiece with his hand and said to me, "They will be asking you questions, like they did on the night Old Pilgrim Church burned."

I looked up at him. His expression turned dark with suspicion and disbelief. He leaned in, nailing me with his gaze. "Elijah, did you have anything to do with *that*?"

"No, Dad."

"You know *nothing* about it?"

There I went mute, because I did have suspicions about Mr. Dowland. I gulped.

"Elijah, look me in the eye and tell me you know nothing about that fire."

"It wasn't me!"

Dad was back to the phone. "Yes, Darrell? This is Russell Creek, at the camp. Can you swing by at your earliest convenience? My son has made a discovery, and we're going to need your help. We'll be in my office." He paused. "Well, according to Elijah, it's a human skeleton."

He hung up the phone slowly, considering it for a minute. His eyes slid to me. His voice was stern. "Start at the beginning, Elijah. And I mean the *very* beginning."

Chapter 11

MY story to Dad was a pretty confusing mess. I explained about us going to the library and how no one owned the land, and that we were looking for buried treasure and found a broken compass. I threw in a few more facts here and there, how two pieces of the treasure had Greek words on them, which meant a big mystery. And that those were stolen, but we weren't giving up the search.

I knew it sounded idiotic. Who could cover three months of adventure in three minutes? As I said before, I'm more a man of action than a man of words.

As the cruiser pulled up, I rushed to the part where Skid almost fell in the well. I mentioned about scientists coming to Mei's house and taking an old belt to have it tested.

"So Mei's parents know about this . . . but you didn't tell *your mother and me?*"

I shook my head. "They don't know anything. The scientists only talked about it with us. Mei's mom didn't see the belt or hear anything about our quest."

"And these . . . these scientists were aware that none of your parents knew what you were doing?"

"They told us to keep it secret."

He got all ruffled. "Oh, I don't like the sound of this!"

Officer Taylor was coming up the steps.

"Dad, you can't tell the police about the treasure. They wouldn't understand. What if news got out and everybody in the county went combing the countryside and digging around camp here for priceless artifacts?!"

"Let me handle it, son."

Dad let me call Skid and Robbie while he talked to Officer Taylor outside. I explained that the police were here, that we were going back to the ruin. I told them to lay low and not say anything to anyone about the skeleton or the armor until they heard from me.

Dad and I drove to Council Cliffs State Park behind the cruiser. As we pulled in at the entrance, Dad said, "Here's what I told Officer Taylor: that you boys had been treasure hunting and had dug up a broken compass which pointed in the direction of the ruin. That one of you accidentally had stepped on the hole, which was covered by rotten wood, and discovered the remains. Is that the truth?"

"Yes."

We parked near a picnic area. My feelings were all mixed up. I was glad I wasn't keeping anything from Dad anymore, glad he was dealing with the police. But the secret of the armor had now spread to one more person. By the time news got out about the body in the well, questions would be flying all over town.

Reece and Mei had to be told. If I knew my parents at all, they'd be setting up a meeting with the other moms and dads to hash things out.

I could feel the belt of truth slipping through my fingers.

I cut through the woods the same way as before, with Officer Taylor and Dad following. In about an hour, we were at the edge of the meadow. I showed Officer Taylor the dog remains first because it was still stinking to high Heaven and hard to ignore. I admitted that the arrows lodged in his body were mine, and I showed them the hole where I'd pulled out the one. I don't mind saying that both Dad and Officer Taylor were very impressed with my marksmanship.

"It happened on our first trip. He came from up there," I pointed to Devil's Cranium. "He saw us and came tearing down across the meadow. If I hadn't decided at the last minute to take my bow, we'd have had no way to protect ourselves. Skid had the shovel, but it wouldn't have been enough."

With the back of his hand across his nose, Dad studied the bug-eaten body. He frowned, heaved a couple of big sighs, turned me toward himself, and gave me a hug. Then he looked over my head toward the hills and frowned and blinked and squeezed my shoulder.

"The well's over there," I said, and led them to it.

Officer Taylor shone his flashlight down into the hole a long while. He shook his head and groaned. I guess no matter how much crime you see—though in Magdeline there isn't much murder and gore—if you're a good solid person like Officer Taylor, it still gets to you.

He started writing in a little notebook. He and Dad decided that the deceased had been dead a long time, years maybe. They exchanged guesses about the depth of the well. Officer Taylor remembered some fuel company coming into town a long time ago to dig for natural gas, though only a few pockets were ever found. He wondered if this was a drilling site. But they both thought the walls of the hole looked more like stonework than bedrock. The location next to a farmhouse seemed logical for a well. He studied the old wood planks awhile, asked me how Skid happened to fall through. The department would have to bring in special equipment to get the remains out, he said.

We walked around the ruin, Officer Taylor asking more questions, me answering every one with the absolute truth.

"You were here looking for treasure, you said?" asked Officer Taylor.

"Yes, sir. We had a metal detector, but all we found were some metal pieces that had fallen off the house."

"Do you know anything about this?" He nodded to a pile of ashes on the front stoop.

"Yes, sir. Our first time here, I built a fire to heat water for hot chocolate."

"So you were here twice."

"Yes, sir. We didn't find anything the first time. But the compass pointed here, so we thought we'd missed a clue and came back for one more look."

"You're quite the outdoorsman, aren't you?" he asked with a smile.

"I learned a lot from my dad." I smiled back and felt a little easier.

"And where is this compass you found?"

"I think Robbie has it. I can get it for you—and whatever else you need, as soon as we get back."

"Good. Did you boys camp out here?"

"No, sir. Both times we were here for just a couple of hours."

I paused at this point, because I figured this next bit of information would complicate things, but I'd promised myself to tell the whole truth, as much as I could. (I should say here that if you are ever questioned by the police, always tell the truth. They have ways of getting it out of you, one way or the other. They're trained to tell if you're lying.)

"By the way, there were five of us the first time, not three."

"Five of you?" asked Officer Taylor.

"Five?" Dad repeated.

"Yeah. Mei and Reece came with us." I prepared for an explosion and it came.

"Reece?!" Dad's voice cut through me. "You brought Reece all the way out here!" He explained to Officer Taylor, "That's Reece Elliston, a classmate of his. Little blond girl who walks with a limp." He scowled at me. "Elijah, I can't believe you'd—" he broke off, scanning the meadow and surrounding hills.

"She really wanted to come, Dad. I was worried too. I wanted to back out of it, but she never gets to have adventures."

"Which way did you come?" he asked, perplexed.

The truth was getting pricklier and pricklier. I felt my face going hot.

"Elijah, how did the five of you get here?" Dad persisted.

My words came in a rush. "We took the golf cart through Owl Woods and walked the rest of the way. She really wanted to be on the treasure hunt, Dad. And her mom said she could go hiking. Reece promised her mom that I could take care of her—me and Skid and Robbie. And we did."

Officer Taylor headed back toward the well, radioing headquarters with the news. But Dad wasn't through with me yet. Getting his bearings between the spot where we stood and where the camp was, he fixed his eyes on Devil's Cranium with an expression of disbelief and anger. "You didn't bring her down that cliff?"

"It was the only way."

"Son, do you realize how risky that was? If she had fallen . . ."

"Us guys were there all around her, every single step."

"Her mother would be furious if she knew you brought her down a cliff! Elijah, you know better than that!"

"It was the only way we knew to get down! We couldn't go through the Morgan farm. That would be trespassing, not to mention their Black Angus bulls! And actually, Dad, it turned out for the best because, if we'd left her up there, Salem would have got her for sure."

"Salem?" Dad's eyes turned suspicious again. "Who's Salem?"

I nodded to the carcass, my heart sinking. "That was his name."

Chapter 12

REECE might believe that the truth will set you free, but all I got was grounded.

When Officer Taylor had finished questioning me, we hiked back through the park. He said he'd be in touch. Dad and I went back to his office for more privacy. I explained about Salem and Mr. Dowland: how I suspected that the old ex-preacher and alleged arsonist was crazy and had set fire to Old Pilgrim Church and then set his vicious dog loose on me while my scent was still fresh in his nose.

Dad sat there, leaning back in his chair, one arm crossed in front of him, the other hand gripping his chin for dear life, all kinds of worries and scoldings working around in his head, though he never said a thing until I was done.

I said again that I was really, truly sorry, but we kids had promised each other to keep the treasure hunt a secret, never having any idea it would come to all this. He asked about the scientists again, and I admitted that, yes, the Stallards did know the whole story. But they were the only adults who knew, and they had agreed to keep it to themselves.

Dad didn't trust them. "Elijah, responsible adults don't tell children to keep secrets from their parents. Did you think about that at all?"

"It was Skid's idea," I continued. Suddenly I felt sick about giving them the belt of truth—them in their safari outfits, probably off to Tanzania or Morocco, where we'd never hear from them again. Who from Chicago wears clothes like that anyway?

"His parents know them," I defended. "That's why I thought it was okay."

"Well, I'm having a talk with all involved. And you—" he stood and heaved a sigh, "are staying home. This grounding will be until further notice. It's as much for your safety as anything. You'll come home right after school and help me at the camp."

"Okay," I said cautiously, waiting for the other shoe to drop.

He studied me a long moment, gave a dry chuckle, and softened a little. "Actually, the timing's pretty good. I'm going to need your help with those high school guys from Mad River Boys Ranch."

"Help?" My stomach felt uneasy again.

He shoved his hands in his pockets, looking like Skid in the way he carried himself. "I feel sorry for those boys. Their families have given up on them, labeled them incorrigible. But we have to watch them like hawks." He looked at the calendar on his desk. "It'll be a good lesson for you, Elijah: to see what happens when you break faith with your parents." He came from behind his desk and wrapped his arms around me. I hugged him back and felt tons better.

We headed out the door. He turned back to lock it. "Elijah, you have made some risky choices, bad choices perhaps—the biggest one being hiding the truth from me. But I understand why you did most of it. Promises are important." He considered me with an expression that looked like admiration. "The way you protected your friends from that dog, Elijah, was quite—" his voice kind of cracked, "quite heroic."

"I didn't have a choice, Dad. I had to do something."

Mom and Dad were worried about my safety. They made it clear I wouldn't know a whole lot of what was going on with the investigation. But Dad would stay in contact with Officer Taylor and promised to keep me informed.

Dad said Mr. Dowland had been questioned about his dog. He'd claimed it accidentally got loose one day and never came back. I had my doubts about the "accidentally" part.

Three dark clouds were now hovering over my life: the investigation, the Mad River Boys, and the twins.

Mom had baby-sitting dibs on me. Every year she and her friends organize the school's annual Christmas Village and Breakfast with Santa. They buy up a ton of cheap presents: key rings and picture frames, coffee mugs and doilies. Then they throw together a pretend village in the band room for a day of shopping frenzy where kids can buy Christmas presents for their friends and families. There's always caroling and a pancake breakfast going on the whole time, after which the kids' choir performs out in the commons. Somewhere in there—surprise, surprise—Santa pops in with bags of candy.

As Mom rushed out of the house on Saturday, she said, "By

the way, Elijah, I volunteered you as stage manager for the choir performance. Miss Flewharty likes your work."

· For the next three hours, the twins had their own personal monkey bars: me. It was fun for a while. But to save my skin from being rubbed off, I said, "Okay, let's play grapevine." I tied a rope from the railing of our loft for them to swing on. Mom says swinging over furniture on a rope is a bad idea and can only lead to broken bones or lamps. But it hasn't yet.

The twins were due to turn seven on Friday the thirteenth. They bugged me about getting them presents.

I said. "Your birthday is bad luck! And get this: in some Indian tribes twins are a bad omen and are taken into the woods and smothered with moss!" (Most Indian stuff is really cool, but not all of it is rational.)

"Nuh-uh!" said Nori, the darker, strong-willed one.

"I'm telling Mom you scared me," whimpered Stacy, her little face all eyes surrounded by brown fluff.

"Tell on me and you get no more grapevines," I threatened.

Nori snickered. "Then we'll lingle you!"

I'd only been able to decode a few words of the twins' secret language over the years: *rinken-rascal* meant "bully," for one. And I knew about their imaginary pets, the lobbies, because the twins were always leaving bowls of weeds around the camp as food for them. You'd think they'd catch on when the food never disappears that lobbies don't exist, but it never mattered to them.

Lingle, I pondered. *Whatever that means, it can't be good.*

Chapter 13

THE newspaper story about the investigation was sketchy, saying only that remains were found "in a remote spot west of Council Cliffs State Park." It didn't say who found them, which was fine with me. I figured my dad had a hand in keeping my name out of it. The less everyone knew, the better.

But little good that did. That very Monday, Justin Brill shot off his big fat mouth in the school hallway. "Hey, Creek, you were out there where they found the body, weren't you?" He followed me to my locker. "My brother said he drove you and Skid and Robbie to the park and you headed west with a shovel."

"So?" I said.

"So did you guys find it?"

I shrugged. "What if we did?"

"Cool! Hey guys, Nature Boy found the dead guy! Hey, what did it look like?"

I shoved books into the locker and pulled books out, not thinking about which ones I needed for the next class. I just wanted to get out of there. Half a dozen of Brill's buddies surrounded me, firing questions like, "How did you know it was there?" "Who clued you in?" "Was it gross?" "Who is it?"

They were thinking and acting exactly how I would have, if I hadn't seen it myself. But after that first horror of discovery, a quiet, creeping isolation had settled in around me. I couldn't imagine dying like that. To be honest, I couldn't imagine dying at all, although my little run-in with Salem had given me a glimpse into the possibility.

I'd been viewing my life differently since finding the skeleton in the well.

Slamming my locker, I turned to face them. "Look, somebody died, and nobody knew about it for years. It's not funny, guys."

"Well, woo-hoo," said Justin, backing off a little. "Hey, we just want to know what it looked like. Was it all bones, or was there rotting flesh, or what?"

I pushed past them and headed down the hall. Justin and his gang sauntered after me, saying stuff about how I was "in good" with the cops now. And how they'd need to watch out when I was around. I turned the corner in a rush and almost ran right into Reece.

"Hey," I said.

"How've you been?" she asked.

"I've got to get to class," I muttered and hurried on.

I felt bad about pushing her off like that, so I spent second lunch choking down cold mushroom pizza and writing her a note.

She came over to my desk in pre-algebra. I couldn't tell

if she was hurt or mad. "What's going on with you?" she whispered. "Why won't you talk to me?"

"I can't." I handed the note to her. "This explains everything."

She took it to her desk and started reading:

Reece,

Sorry. I was getting away from Brill and his gang. I guess it's all over school about how Skid, Robbie, and I found the dead body at the ruin. I'm grounded. I can't talk about it even over the phone because of the investigation. But I need to ask you other stuff. Has my dad or mom called your mom yet? Things are pretty strange at home. Be sure to volunteer for Christmas Village. You'd make a good elf. We can talk there.

E—

She flashed me a smile.

After school I baby-sat, and at night I helped with the Mad River Boys.

I wouldn't generally be uneasy about hanging out with high school guys, even ones who go by names like Blade and D-Day. To each his own. But they had criminal records. They'd been hauled off to the ranch because their parents couldn't handle them or didn't want them anymore. They were in the care—if you could call it that—of Lafe, a burly red-haired guy always flexing his fingers, like he was working up to strangling somebody.

Dad had bribed the boys with a promise of winter kayaking

at the end—if they behaved. I was warned I'd have to help chaperone. In the meantime I did night duty, 8:00 to 11:00 P.M. The Mad River Boys had already torn up a couple of bunks the first night. They'd snuck out to smoke, thrown hot coals on each other, filled the foosball table with pop to make a "lake," and tried to run some raggedy undershorts up the flagpole—with the kid still in them. If I could catch them in the act of tearing up one more thing, Dad might send them home, and I wouldn't have to risk my life on the icy waters of Deer Creek.

Night watch also gave me time to ponder all sorts of unanswered questions. From the upstairs office in the lodge, with the lights off and using high-powered binoculars, I could see the open areas of the camp. The moon was full, the trees bare. I could even see through Owl Woods almost to Great Oak.

Camp Mudjokivi was beautiful at night in late fall—like a charcoal drawing on dark paper, with streams of chalk-white moonlight on the lake, and a dark purple sky dotted with stars. The cabin lights on the far hillside made little squares of gold on the dark landscape.

I edged open the window, letting in a stream of cold air. It was the only way I'd hear any goings-on. Compared to summer days when trees are thick and green, when lawn mowers buzz and swimmers squeal and team whistles blow, camp on a winter night is lonely and delicate, silent and fine.

I checked in with Bo on the walkie-talkies every so often, focused my binoculars on the far cabins where the Mad River Boys were staying, and watched.

My dad had gone to a lot of trouble to make Camp Mudj a safe place for kids. For that reason he always scheduled the Boys' meals and activities apart from the rest of the campers. They hounded the counselors all the time about riding the golf carts, and eyed me like a pack of hungry coyotes when I drove around the lake to haul paint to the Tree House Village. Dad dreaded this week all year, but we needed the business if we were going to expand.

The bird clock sounded the coo of a mourning dove: 10:00. Night watch worked a spell on me; minutes ticked by slowly. I thought dark, random thoughts. *What would people think of Camp Mudj if news got out about dead bodies near the property, about criminal boys in the back cabins, about man-eating dogs running loose, about Russ Creek's own son prowling the countryside looking for buried treasure?*

Why did the compass point to the well, and not to the next piece of armor? If the compass was our last clue, how can our quest go on? Where is the broken compass anyway? Last time I saw it, it was in Robbie's hand at Mei's house. I need to turn it over to Officer Taylor.

Where are the Stallards, and what are they doing with our belt of truth?

Who is that person at the bottom of the well; and did he have anything to do with Old Pilgrim Church?

I stuck on that last question, chewing it over. Dowland had said that things happened right before the church died all those years ago. As he put it, "Another terrible thing swept through the church, a thing that can't be explained by common sense, *a thing no family should ever have to go through*."

Maybe that person at the bottom of the well was a member of his church. Could Dowland have wanted someone to find the body, so it could be put in a grave and finally rest in peace? I needed to call Reece and ask her opinion, but I couldn't leave my post. I wasn't supposed to talk to anyone about the case except Mom and Dad, Robbie and Skid until further notice. I sat there in the cold and dark, thinking about questions with no answers.

A chill ran through me, not from the cold draft. *Was Dowland lying about Salem, lying to protect the armor . . . lying . . . just like me?*

Chapter 14

THINGS were looking up. I was only ninety-five percent grounded. My previous work on *The Adventures of Tom Sawyer* had scored points with Miss Flewharty and Mrs. Coyle, so I was officially a Christmas Village stagehand. It was as good an excuse as any to get out of the house. I asked Mei if she wanted to use her talent painting the village backdrop. Robbie and Reece signed up to be elves. They'd be selling junk in the village and passing out candy for Santa.

And one of my dark clouds was passing: it was the last day of camp for the Mad River Boys. They didn't deserve the winter kayak trip, after chalking up $612 in damages. But Dad felt sorry for them. He knew that when they got on the bus to leave, a few of them would bawl like babies.

I had to go along. Dad and Bo and Lafe were big strong men, but the Boys outnumbered them four to one. Counting me it was three to one, not much better. There was no way of telling how it would go. Either they had learned something about good sportsmanship from camp, or they'd see the kayak trip down Deer Creek as one last chance to go hog-wild.

The afternoon was cold with a white fog still heavy in the valleys. Mom made me wear layers and pack a change of clothes in a plastic bag . . . "just in case."

I figured my fate was sealed as tight as that bag.

On the half-hour bus ride to Deer Creek, the Boys made it clear they were never going to like me. Maybe they were jealous of the cool setup I had. They'd hounded me all week about driving the golf cart. Dad had coached me to say, "Sorry, guys. Camp policy," and keep moving. But one night the lock of the maintenance garage was jimmied. The Mad River Boys didn't like taking no for an answer.

While Dad was lining up the kayaks, Leon slipped up behind me and said in a creepy, threatening voice: "I know things about nature. I know that if you catch a cicada and yank off its legs, its head pops right off too. *Pop!*"

Dad made them listen to me talk about kayak safety. They just snickered and nodded knowingly to each other. I was sure I was doomed.

We floated down Deer Creek, Bo and Dad doing their nature spiels, the Boys not paying much attention.

D-Day paddled up beside me. "Hey, kid, do you have any sisters?"

When I ignored the question, he jabbed my kayak with his oar. "What do you do for fun around here?"

They all laughed at my answer: hiking and helping with the camp. What I liked best was practicing with my bow and arrow, but I thought it best to keep weapons out of the conversation.

They wanted to know who lived in the other cabins. "Nobody," I said. "They're rentals for campers."

All afternoon they griped, one guy's temper setting off another:

"This is boring."

"You're boring, Javier. Shut up."

"Both of you shut up!"

"Who stole my water bottle? Leon?"

"C. T. did."

"You're dead, C."

"He's a lying—"

"I'll kill ya.'"

Lafe broke in. "I'll dump you all and hold you under till you're blue and bloated."

Maybe it was just their way of getting along. I don't know. But it got on Dad's nerves big time.

I'd learned years ago that when tomcats get in a fight—tearing around the neighborhood bothering people—you can sometimes shut them all up by hitting one in the gut with a big rock.

I don't mind saying it crossed my mind.

Watching for one to slip out of the pack and escape or fracture another's skull with a paddle, I kept my distance from the Mad River Boys as much as possible. I'd maneuver close to Bo, who's built like a world-class wrestler—or I'd move up behind Dad who's tall and knows how to put a commanding edge to his voice. But I steered clear of Lafe.

I actually missed having Skid around. I could have used the moral support.

We'd gotten off fairly easy with the Mad River Boys, I thought. Javier got a good enough whack with his paddle to flip C. T. into Deer Creek, but at least it wasn't me.

Building a good campfire was the last lesson, and not a moment too soon. The Boys were starving for hot dogs, and C. T.'s lips were blue. Leon went with him back to the bus to get him a change of clothes.

We should have known better.

I demonstrated how to place the tinder, the kindling, then the logs. When it was their turn, they did it all wrong on purpose, bunching up the kindling too tight, using wet wood. I tried to help but they cussed and yelled, "Lay off!"

Okay, fine! I thought. *That sickly fire will never take off.*

It was barely hot enough to roast one hot dog, much less twelve. They crowded into a circle and pushed their sticks into the measly fire, getting ashes all over their hot dogs and marshmallows, fighting for the hottest spot. The flames sputtered. Dad and Bo went looking for dry tinder. Lafe already had disappeared into the woods. The boys were carping about "raw" hot dogs, when Leon eased up beside me in the circle.

"Just taking care of business," he said wickedly. He was hiding something under his jacket. I got a whiff of gasoline. Out came a paper cup; in a flash I knew he'd siphoned gas out of the bus.

"No!!!" I yelled, but it was too late. He'd already flung fuel across the wood.

Whhhfff! A pillar of fire ten feet wide billowed out. The Boys fell back, whooping and cussing. I felt the blast of heat as flames rolled up into the sky.

For a second, they thought it was cool. But when the pillar of fire dissolved into the trees, the Boys were faced with the remains of their dinners: shriveled, black wads of char on the ends of their smoldering sticks.

They looked stunned.

I threw my head back and laughed and kept on laughing until Dad and Bo came running. "It's okay," I said. "Leon decided to help the fire along."

Dad fumed silently for a moment. Then his frown slowly changed to a grin. He turned to me with an expression of sweet revenge. "Looks like somebody's going home hungry."

We loaded them on the bus. D-Day called me a name and said something I can't repeat. As their bus drove off, he gave me the wickedest smile. But there were a few in the bunch who cried and wanted to stay. The look on Dad's face told me they'd be invited back next year.

When the bus had disappeared, Dad and Bo blew out lungfuls of air and shook hands. Bo threw out his arms like an umpire and yelled, "Safe!" He punched me and said, "Thanks, kid."

There wasn't much to like about the Mad River Boys. But I couldn't help thinking that, if Leon had wanted to pay me back for having a better life than him, he could have given me a shove into that pillar of fire, and I'd have ended up a black wad of char.

Chapter 15

IT was the first of December and surprises were still coming in twos. First there were two Dr. Stallards, when we thought there was only one. And as it turned out—when the police got their equipment back to the ruin—they found two skeletons in that hole: a woman and a baby.

When I came in from school, Mom was looking at the newspaper. Nori and Stacy were coloring at the kitchen table. Mom put a finger to her lips and let me look at the headline: Remains of Two Found at Site.

We weren't supposed to talk about it at dinner, but Nori brought up the subject, even before the chili was dipped. She wriggled into her chair and looked over at me.

"Tara said you found two skeletons in a well."

So much for small-town secrets.

Mom passed her a bowl. "Cheese and crackers and carrot sticks are on the table, girls. Don't take more than you'll eat. That story you heard is a matter for the police. It's nothing you need to talk about with your friends at school." She murmured to Dad, "I can't believe people discuss things like this in front of their babies."

Nori studied her bowl a minute, then looked back at me. "Did you?"

"Yeah," I said.

Mom shot me a look.

"I did. I'm not going to lie about it." Then I turned to Nori, "But that's all I'm going to say."

"Did a bad guy kill them?" Stacy asked, her voice small and squeaky.

Mom smoothed Stacy's wavy hair. "Whatever happened took place years ago, sweetheart. It's not for us to be concerned about."

It was Dad's turn. "We don't know that they *were* killed. How was your day at school, Nori?"

"Where is the deep hole?" Stacy asked.

"It's way far away," Mom said. "You don't need to worry."

"Maybe they fell in and died," Nori said to Stacy cheerfully, "and nobody killed them!"

I said, "Or . . . maybe they had a big brother named Elijah, and they asked him too many questions and he went berserk." I grabbed Nori, pulled her off the chair, and pretended to beat on her. Not to be left out, Stacy piled on us right there on the kitchen floor. Mom knew I was trying to distract them, so I didn't get the usual viper stare.

After dinner Dad brought me into the living room. He showed me the newspaper article, and we read it together. Dad asked me about what Dowland said when I went to his house.

I ran to my room and got my notes, hidden in my quiver hanging on the wall so the twins wouldn't find it.

Dad sat down and read it over. "This part where he talks

about terrible things happening . . . did he go into any detail?"

"No. That's all I know. Bad things happened at the church before it closed down, was all he said."

"May I show your notes to the police?" he asked.

I tried to stay calm. "Well, it tells all about the armor, and I wanted to keep that quiet."

"I understand that, but you may have some very important information here."

I sat on the ottoman in front of him. "Can I rewrite it and leave the armor parts out?"

"The police will want to know why you went to Mr. Dowland's house."

The problem of telling the truth cropped up again. Truth ends up being so narrow sometimes. What I mean is, I could make up a zillion reasons why I went to Dowland's that day. But there's really only one *true* answer.

"Son," Dad said in an even voice, "I don't think they really will care about an old suit of armor that once stood in a church." He went on carefully, like he didn't want to hurt my feelings. "It's not a priceless artifact. Mr. Dowland said so himself; it's a trinket. And this nonsense of it being cursed—you're smarter than that, Elijah."

"I just don't want anyone else looking for it," I said. "Finding it means a lot to me . . . and the others."

Dad leaned back and sighed tiredly. Dark circles under his eyes told me he had clouds hanging over him too. He said,

"I can't see the police taking any interest in it, since it has nothing to do with the death of this lady and her child."

"But I think it does, Dad. Why else would the belt be buried with a compass that pointed to the well?"

He was stumped and gave me long thoughtful look. "You're a smart kid, you know that?"

"Yeah, I know."

We grinned.

I asked him, "Since the belt was buried with the compass, would it be evidence?"

He looked puzzled. "It could be."

"But the belt is in Chicago, you know. The Stallards would have to make a special trip to bring it down. That's a lot of trouble for a trinket."

We sat there a long time just looking out the front window at camp. He read my notes again and thoughtfully repeated Dowland's riddle, "'Piece by piece they will rest in peace.' What do you think he meant by that?"

"He's loons, is what I think."

Dad gave me a look. "To call someone loons is disrespectful."

"How about daft? That's Robbie's word."

"How about troubled? He must be a troubled man."

"Loopy?" I teased.

"Troubled!" Dad was grinning.

"Deranged?"

He shook his head at me and laughed. A long, quiet moment

passed. His eyes wandered around the room, then returned to me. "Elijah, I want you to keep this between us just for now, everything we've discussed. I need to think this through."

"Okay."

He said in a low voice, "If this turns out to be a murder, or if Mr. Dowland is involved, then we may have to consider the possibility that all the other pieces of the armor are connected to . . . other crimes."

A chill went down my spine. "You mean other murders?"

"If that's the case—" he bounced my notes in his hand as if to weigh them, "then we must turn this over to the police as is. We don't want to withhold evidence." He looked at the paper, then at me. "This whole affair is bizarre."

"You're telling me. You know, Robbie's real smart with the library. He could check into the history of Old Pilgrim Church and see if anyone died mysteriously after the armor came."

Dad was reading Dowland's story again. "Uh-huh. He said some people died and others moved away."

Another chill followed the first one down my spine. "Whoa . . . what if they didn't move away? What if everyone in town just *thought* they moved away?"

I can hardly describe all the expressions that crossed my dad's face. It started with a stare, his eyes in neutral while his mind considered my idea. Then he suddenly looked right at me—like Dowland did, but not in a scary way—reading every inch of my face, trying to figure out who I was.

I couldn't bring myself to tell him about the vision quest, and how that old "trinket" could very well be the armor of God. He might understand, or he might think I was going off the deep end like Dowland. Deranged. Daft. Loopy.

He was calm and quiet on the surface, but stuff was raging on the inside. I saw a little of myself in his face—deep and thoughtful in the lamplight. I let the sights and sounds of my home all soak in: the clatter of Mom doing dishes, the twins sounding all *skippity-hoppity* in the kitchen, the serious quiet of the living room. A strange feeling of warmth and strength welled up in me.

"Dad?"

"What, son?"

"I'm not giving up on finding every last piece of the armor. I'll wait until the heat dies down, or the murders are solved." I shook my head. "But I'm not giving up. I can't."

"Okay," he said, eyeing me curiously. "We'll play it by ear."

Chapter 16

THANKS to Jeremy Brill, people were feeding on rumors like a school of piranhas.

One grapevine claimed the guys and I had gotten lost, found an old house, and were drawing water from a well when up came a bucket of bones. Another rumor had us digging for a body after a mad dog chased us to a well. Robbie and I stayed to ourselves as much as possible, swearing on our honor we'd keep quiet. "Mum's the word," we'd say to each other. It was hard for Robbie because he's a talker. I didn't see Skid much—our class schedules are pretty opposite—but we crossed paths once and punched our fists together.

"*Daijoubu?*" he asked in Japanese.

"*Daijoubu,*" I said. "Mum's the word."

"*Ganbatte,*" he said back.

Work on the Christmas Village came as welcome relief. In the buzz and whine of woodshop, the shop teacher and I cut out the plywood buildings. Then Mei and Reece showed up to paint. Mrs. Coyle set us up with drop cloths and then left us on our own. She'd given the go-ahead on Mei's cutesy sketches, each storefront a different color. The little kids would go crazy over it. Since senior art students would be doing the detail work, our job was to slap on a coat of color. We propped the wood cutouts against the wall, grabbed brushes, and started in, me in the middle with Reece and Mei on either side, and the sketches stuck to the wall in front of us so we'd get the colors right.

We spent the next hour trying *not* to talk about the mysteries stacking up on us. But the more we tiptoed around the problems, the bigger they got.

"We can't worry about this," said Reece finally. "So here's the drill: we wait for news from the Stallards and keep our eyes open for the next clue. That's it. No panicking, no looking too far ahead. Believe me, that never works."

My guess was Reece had been fighting panic a lot in her life, not knowing whether she'd ever walk right or end up in a wheelchair. When Reece made a comment about big things in life, I tended to listen.

I asked, "So do you have any Bible words for us—" I faked a southern preacher's drawl, "to brang comfurt tew ar trubbled lahves in ar tahm uv need?"

She stopped painting and tipped her head at me, almost like Mom's viper stare. "You should always, *always* leave the acting to Robbie. You sounded like a complete idiot." She went back to painting. "I have a Bible verse for you: 'Then he went away and hanged himself. Go and do likewise.'"

"It doesn't say that in the Bible!" I said, but I was guessing.

"Does too. Both statements are in there," she grinned. "Just . . . not together." She pointed her brush at me. "Gotcha!"

I slopped some aqua paint on her nose. She came back with pink and caught me on the ear. Mei stood there cackling until lilac ran down her arm and dripped off her elbow.

Yeah, it was welcome relief to hang out with them for a while.

Mom and Dad staged a holiday get-together, as they called it. Really it was a chance to meet Skid's parents face-to-face and find out what they knew about the Stallards. The tree was up—decorated with everything from fancy angels to little scraps of sparkly paper the twins had made every year from the time they were in diapers. Some of my creations were on the tree too: a clothespin reindeer, a sled made from ice cream sticks, stuff like that. The house was fixed up as usual for the holidays, with electric candles in the windows and lots of angels and teddy bears in Christmas clothes stacked here and there in the corners.

After being at Mei's house, I wondered what foreigners think of our Christmas decorations: a tree hauled inside with sparkly ropes and things draped on it, girl dolls with wings and satin dresses hanging around with flesh-eating animals dressed in sweaters.

Where do those crazy ideas come from? Beats me.

When Skid's parents stepped into the entryway of our log house, I understood where their son got his coolness. Carlotta Skidmore was Skid's Latino half. She looked like a flamenco dancer in her red dress and red high heels. She had short, dark pixie hair, and a wide smile with lips the color of her dress.

Dominic Skidmore was your basic military man: muscles and posture, iron handshake, buzzed hair, and square jaw. He had Skid's lime green eyes and dark skin. He was half-black, half-white, the other two halves of Marcus Skidmore's three-way genetics.

Aunt Grace and Uncle Dorian came in matching Christmas sweaters and dark slacks. Dad was in a sweater and slacks, casual but nice. Mom looked pretty in a dark green dress, but I could tell she was a little rattled hosting the new people. She'd dropped the girls off at the baby-sitter's so the adults could gab in peace.

We guys didn't dress up.

It wasn't a dinner, but there was still a ton of food. The house smelled of hot cinnamon cider and sausage balls. There were cheese balls with crackers, big plates of vegetables, and Aunt Grace's homemade bread. And eggnog. And cookies.

While the parents got acquainted, we guys piled up plates and went upstairs to my room.

I'd mentioned before about suspecting the twins had surveillance equipment in my room. That night I solved the mystery. There's something about the way the heat ducts and cold air returns are situated, so that if the heat's off and the vents are open, you can hear from other rooms. In certain spots voices come through almost as clear as a bell. We figured it out when we could hear our parents talking downstairs. I shushed the guys. We stopped to listen.

"I bet they're talking about the case," Robbie whispered.

He began to move around the room to track the sound and ended up with his ear to the floor vent, his backside high in the air. I came over to listen.

It's not polite to eavesdrop, but the conversation involved us. We checked the other upstairs vents for the best reception, and ended up in the girls' room. Their vent must have joined the other vents right over the kitchen. With our ears pressed to the opening, we started piecing together the latest news. Robbie ran back to my room for pencil and paper. I'd worked on listening out in nature, so I dictated what I heard.

"Young woman . . . and infant . . . remains of dress and sweater, baby blanket."

"Baby blanket?" Robbie said excitedly. "Remember that piece of rag that we found with the helmet and arm piece? That looked like a blanket. Do you think they're the same?"

"Shh! They may be able to hear us," I said, turning my ear back to the vent.

"Severe blow, suggesting . . ." The rest was muffled.

Our heads met over the vent as they had over the well.

"On impact . . . the baby."

The moms' voices crooned sadly for a while.

"Accident? . . . How can they determine? . . . so many years . . ."

We pieced together that the woman must have died on impact, but that the police couldn't tell if it was an accidental fall or a deliberate push. We also picked up that Mr. Dowland had been questioned and released already, then more mumbling about him, the words *danger* and *troubled*.

The conversation faded to white noise as the parents drifted back to the kitchen counter for seconds on food. I smelled coffee, which signaled dessert time.

"Want some cookies?" I asked. We headed down the steps with our empty plates.

"That coffee gives me an idea," Skid said.

"What?" Robbie asked.

Skid stopped us at the bottom of the stairs. "You know where we can *really* get the scoop?"

"Where?" I asked.

"Florence's."

Robbie's face screwed up like he'd been punched in the stomach. Florence's: where the R.O.M.E.O. (Really Old Men Eating Out) Club hangs out, the greasy spoon where no self-respecting kid would be caught dead or alive.

"Can't," I said with relief. "I'm grounded."

Skid said, "Robbie and I can still go."

Robbie's face perked up. It would be just him and Skid hanging out together. *Without me.*

"I'll try to get out of it," I said, hardly believing I'd risk getting re-grounded for a meal in Florence's.

"You shouldn't," Skid said.

"No, you shouldn't," Robbie echoed.

"Wouldn't hurt to ask," I headed for the food.

Lounging around back in my room, we discussed timing. "How about Sunday morning?"

Skid shook his head. "I do church."

"Then Saturday?" I suggested.

"It has to be early," Skid said. "Senior citizens don't sleep much."

"Yeah, when Grandma comes, she's up at the crack."

"Crack o' dawn then," Skid decided.

When the company left and mom had gone to get the twins, I asked Dad, "So what's the verdict?"

"The Skidmores are really nice people," he said, and I could tell he meant it. We cleared dishes.

"What'd they say about the Stallards?" I asked.

"They really don't know the Stallards that well, and have met Dr. Eloise only a time or two. Dom and Carlotta were both in the military, serving in the Middle East, where they met Dr. Dale. He was on a dig."

I wiped the counter. "They're archaeologists."

"Your mom and I think it's best to meet them as soon as possible. They still have this belt you found?"

"Yeah."

"And are they going to bring it back?"

"They'd better."

Dad handed me a little piece of paper. "Here's their phone number. Why don't you give them a call and see what they've found out?"

"Me? Sure, well, okay. But I've only met them once. Maybe Skid should call."

I looked at the number while Dad shoved leftovers into the refrigerator.

"Dad, could I go with Skid and Robbie out to breakfast, so we can talk about it?"

He thought a little more. "Where?"

"Florence's. Tomorrow."

He laughed. "Do kids hang out there now?"

"No," I said sarcastically. "That's the point!"

He shut the refrigerator door and stood looking at me for a while. "Are kids at school giving you a hard time?" Before I could answer, he said, "I didn't think about that. You have a lot to process, don't you?"

I said, "Uh-huh," though I didn't get exactly what he meant.

"Well . . . if you go straight there and straight back. And clear it with Mom first."

"Thanks! You're awesome!" I popped up on a counter stool. "Dad, I know I've asked you this before, but did you ever hear who owns Telanoo?"

"The land behind the camp?"

"Yeah, and all the way to Council Cliffs, including the meadow."

"I don't know."

"I think we should find out."

"Okay. It shouldn't be too much of a problem."

Yeah, right, I thought. *That's what I used to think.*

Chapter 17

THE whole idea of sliding into a sticky booth at Florence's and ordering a greasy breakfast was pretty mortifying. Robbie beat me there a few minutes before 7:30, and boy, did he look like a fish out of water, sitting there at a table and gripping the bottle of ketchup.

"You look like what the cat dragged in," I joked and slid in across from him.

"And what the kittens wouldn't eat," he agreed with a wimpy smile.

The waitress came over and asked what us "young 'uns" wanted. I sat up straight and said in a formal voice that we'd be waiting to order until our *third party* arrived. We sat there on ripped red vinyl chairs, looking at stained paper menus.

Robbie heaved a sigh of relief when Skid came. I sighed too, on the inside.

Skid cased the place. "Let's sit over there." We moved to a booth surrounded by old men in adjoining booths and at a table beside us. Robbie and Skid sat on one side, me on the other. Robbie whispered a joke, "Nothing like being in a geezer sandwich with an order of old men on the side."

The waitress was on her way over when Skid leaned in, "Don't order the oatmeal, whatever you do. Your best bet is scrambled eggs with grits and bacon."

She took our orders and said, "No more funny business," about our moving around on her.

Robbie kept one ear to the gossip while Skid and I made small talk.

"So," I asked, fiddling with the syrup jar, "when are you going to make your move on Miranda Varner?"

"Make my *move?*" His eyebrows went up.

"Yeah."

He made an uncertain gesture with his hand. "What do you mean?"

"You know . . . make your *move?*"

"Like what, tackling her in the school hallway?"

"No, jerk! When are you going to let her know that you like her?"

He crossed his arms and grinned like a sly cat. "She knows."

"Yeah? Well, don't you want to make it official?"

Skid shook his head. "You Americans."

Robbie sat up. "*You're* an American . . . *aren't* you?"

I knew what he meant right away. An army brat like Skid was a man of the world, whereas Robbie and I were corn-fed Ohioans.

Skid shook his head. "You guys treat romance like it's the Indy 500."

We must have looked blank.

He leaned in, resting his elbow on the table, "Okay, here's the lowdown on the current guy-girl thing, as I see—"

"Shhh—" Robbie said and nodded behind him.

We got quiet. A voice behind Skid said, " . . . found the bones at the old Theobald place."

I couldn't believe it when Skid threw one arm across the back of his booth and piped up, "The old Theobald place, huh? Is that what it's called?" He took the Romeos by surprise. They stared. He went on. "You're talking about the recent investigation."

Three old men in different stages of hair loss and all wearing plaid shirts fixed their eyes on us. (I got the strangest feeling that we were pretty much looking at ourselves in sixty years.) The one with his back to our booth groaned and strained to get his rickety body hauled around until he had us in his sights.

"Haven't you been in here before, sonny?" he asked Skid.

"A couple of times," Skid said. "I like the grits."

They all nodded approvingly. One bared his yellow teeth.

Skid reached his hand over the booth awkwardly and shook hands.

"It was some boys who found those bones," said the one old man nearest to us.

"That would be us," Skid continued.

They reared back. "You don't say?"

"This is Elijah and this is Robbie," Skid said.

We exchanged niceties. Their names were Charlie, Obie, and Walter.

"We have to stay out of the loop because we're kids," Skid said smoothly, "in case we're talking crime here. But you gentlemen have the history; you know what there is to know. We were wondering about who owned that farm where the remains were found."

We hardly noticed when our food came.

Obie, bald as a cue ball, twisted himself into a pretzel to see us, and did most of the talking. "Years ago, boys, Old Pilgrim wanted to buy that meadow as a location for a new building—the preacher's idea—in hopes of growing."

"The preacher?" I asked innocently.

"Stan Dowland," he said.

"They planned to put a road in and everything," said Walter, the round, red-faced one with the yellow teeth.

"But the owner wouldn't sell off the meadow without selling off the scrub land with it."

Skid and Robbie looked at me. We all thought the same thing: *Telanoo.*

"Al Theobald," said Charlie, a hangdog man with a comb-over starting behind his ear.

Robbie leaned to me and whispered, "That was his name on the land plats, Alfred Theobald."

"But it was sold!" I whispered back.

Skid gave us the eye. We shut up and listened.

Obie took over the story again, "Oh, they haggled and fought, I recall. But the preacher got his way and the church went ahead."

The waitress came by to give the old men refills. We asked if we could have some coffee too, and turned our cups over.

"They paid more than it was worth," said Charlie.

"Big debt for a little church," said Walter.

They argued whether the loan was borrowed from First Federal or from Theobald himself. I didn't care.

"When church attendance fell off, the money stopped flowing," Obie went on. "Theobald called in his lawyers and the land was foreclosed."

"Foreclosed?" Robbie asked.

"They canceled the deal. Theobald threatened to sue the church if he didn't get his money," said Obie.

"You can sue a church?" I asked. All this church stuff was new to me.

"Things weren't so cut-and-dried back then, boys. A little country church like that didn't bother to get incorporated as a lot of 'em do nowadays. There was an uproar all over town. Theobald didn't want that land. He'd tried to unload it for years. He wanted the money. Anyhow, the church lost it all."

"So who owns it?" I asked, hardly believing I finally was going to find out!

They scratched their heads. They swilled coffee and mopped up gravy. They frowned at each other.

Obie said, "Well, a board of trustees would have to sign for the deed. But they didn't have trustees at Old Pilgrim. Harking back to the old days, I recall a couple of the head men passing away during the fracas."

Charlie turned to Walter. "Wasn't that when Harry Goodman passed? Does that ring a bell with you?"

Walter shook his head and chuckled, "I don't have much of a bell to ring."

Obie went on. "When it came right down to it . . . I'm thinking the preacher was left holding the bag."

"So Stan Dowland owns Tela—I mean, that old farm?"

More head scratching. Charlie said, "If memory serves me, he begged Theobald and First Federal to hold off retaking it."

"Oh, Dowland begged all right. He groveled, but they wouldn't budge," said Obie.

"A messy turn of events," Charlie said. "So let this be a lesson, boys: always get it in writing."

"Wasn't that banker's son sweet on Dowland's girl for a while?" Obie asked. "Wasn't that part of the whole ugly business, Walter?"

"It was Theobald's son," corrected Charlie.

After an exchange of words, they agreed. My neck got tight, waiting for the answer. We all were feeling the strain, but I took cues from Skid and kept listening with interest.

Obie said, "Dowland put a stop to that romance, don't you know? She left town, and soon after that, her mother followed suit. Then Dowland left. When the wife died, he moved back, but not into Magdeline. He got a little place over in Newpoint."

"Who put a stop to what?" Robbie asked.

"The preacher put a stop to his daughter marrying Theobald's boy," Obie said before sloshing down the rest of his cup. "A sad thing it was to see the church fold."

Charlie rumbled. His jowls quivered. "Dowland pushed. He soured 'em all. You don't push people around here. They have to go their own pace."

"It's still called the Theobald place?" I asked.

"That's what it was called *before:* the Theobald place," Obie said.

"What's it called now?" Skid asked.

He reared back and gaped at us like we didn't have the sense God gave a duck. He barked, "Why, the *old* Theobald place!"

"But . . . but after all that died down, who ended up with it?" I asked once more.

"I don't know who'd want it anyhow, that hard, clay dirt," Charlie said. "The Morgan farm, now that's good land, and he's kept it up."

"But who bought that land after Old Pilgrim Church?" I asked. "Who owns it now?"

They shrugged. Obie said, "Don't know. Dowland got stuck with it, I suppose."

"First Federal took it back, I think," suggested Charlie.

"That's right," said Walter. "But that bank closed."

"Then nobody, I guess."

A silence fell.

Skid said, "Thanks, men. We appreciate your time."

Obie turned back to his breakfast.

Robbie's wide eyes fell on me in pure awe. "It *really is* the land no one owns."

"It really is *Telanoo*," I said mysteriously.

Skid took a casual sip of coffee. "Whatever. I guess we're in the clear about trespassing."

I left that morning full of cold grits and bacon, with an old question answered, several new ones sprouting, and a sudden, uncontrollable urge to call on Mr. Dowland once more. But only with Dad's permission. And a bodyguard—maybe Skid. We could go together, and on the way he could finish explaining about the current guy-girl situation and what he planned to do, Miranda-wise.

Chapter 18

I cornered Reece at the water fountain before first class period. I was a bundle of excited nerves.

"I have to get the group together. I think we're onto something."

"What?"

"I may have figured it out."

"What figured out?"

"Who it was . . . out there at the ruin."

She grabbed my wrist. "Elijah! You're kidding!" She smiled at me. "I knew you could solve it. If anyone could . . ."

I pulled her around the corner to a little niche between rows of lockers, out of the flow of traffic. "I couldn't sleep all night, thinking about it. Here it is: Old Pilgrim Church tried to buy that place—the Theobald place, it's called—around the time the church started going under, the same time the armor came. Dowland's church couldn't pay for the land and there was this legal problem between them and Theobald and the bank. Dowland ended up stuck with the problem. Somewhere in there Theobald's son and Dowland's daughter started . . . dating, I guess you could say. Dowland put a stop to it, and his daughter left town and never came back." I paused.

"Okay . . ." she said, waiting for more.

"Do you see what I'm getting at, Reece? *She never came back!*"

It took only a few seconds for it to sink in. Her eyes got wide.

"The one they found in the well . . . was her? And her baby?"

"It makes sense, doesn't it? If Dowland was embarrassed and didn't want the church to know; and if he was fighting over the land; and if his job was in trouble and everybody was jumping ship, what would make him angrier than his daughter and Theobald's son being together?"

Reece went all soft and sad. "Poor Mr. Dowland! Everyone standing back watching to see what the minister would do . . . no one offering to help. Him losing everything."

(I don't know any girl who wouldn't get some kind of sick thrill out of all the romance and death, and a girl being in that kind of trouble. But there was not one glimmer in Reece's expression that this would be fun, juicy stuff to gossip about and roll your eyes over. She's something.)

"How did you figure all this out?" she asked, amazed.

"It was Skid's idea to start with. He made us go to Florence's restaurant for breakfast." I laughed.

"You're kidding!"

"They do have good grits and bacon."

"What're grits?"

"Who knows? Some sort of southern food. But anyhow, the Romeos knew all about the town history, and *we* knew about Dowland's story. We put two and two together."

"You mean to tell me, no one in Magdeline ever put the two stories together, for thirty years?"

"From what we could tell, no one knew where Dowland's daughter went. He kept her whereabouts a secret."

"He was hiding her away there? Or—" her face went pale. "Elijah, do you think he killed her?"

"He's mean, that's for sure. But in that speech to me he said a thing happened that should never happen. That sounds like a freak accident."

"With her baby," Reece whispered. "What if he told everyone she'd left town, but he actually killed her, his *own daughter*, just to hide his shame?"

I checked the hall clock: one minute until the bell. When I turned back, Reece was crying. I stammered and cleared my throat. "Hey, if you need a drink of water or something—" I thumbed at the water fountain, like I was hitching a ride to nowhere. "Dowland's gone off the deep end keeping secrets and lies to himself all these years. He may have forced her into hiding, and she got depressed. Maybe she was running from someone who discovered her, and she fell in."

"No one ever knew . . ." she said, getting sadder by the minute.

"But someone *did* know, Reece. They put boards over the well to hide it."

She glanced down the hall cautiously. "Elijah, if it wasn't an accident, and you're the one who brings it to light, you could be in danger. Real danger! Don't go anywhere by yourself."

I shrugged. "I'll be fine."

With determination she said, "We have to find out what happened to her. We have to uncover the truth."

"That's exactly what I was thinking. The truth."

A feeling washed over me, as if suddenly I wasn't a kid wedged in a hallway at school, but in a much larger place, a place getting bigger and bigger all the time. I saw the belt of truth in my mind's eye: The Ancient Omen. I understood that it was given to me to figure out that finding and keeping the truth is a battle, especially if it's been buried for years. The truth is as hard as granite and tough as nails. The truth can be dangerous. Sometimes getting to it hurts you; you have to brace for it. The proof of that was in Reece's face. But how the truth could set you free—I didn't have the brain space to hold what that could possibly mean.

The clock ticked off another minute. The hallway was nearly empty. "The bell's going to ring," I said. "We've got to get the gang together. But first—first let's me and you go see Dowland."

She sniffed and blinked. "What? Are you crazy!"

"I already told him about you, that the armor means a whole lot to you." A cloud of worry passed over her face, as I backed down the hall toward my class. "One of our parents can take us," I said. "Skid could go as bodyguard."

"I don't know, Elijah. I—"

"Five minutes, that's all we'd need, to see if he'd give us another clue." I called out, getting louder as I went. "Salem's gone and our parents will be right there, so actually we wouldn't need a bodyguard. Actually Skid would intimidate Dowland. Mei wouldn't go. Robbie'd freak out at the very idea, so that leaves you and me." I kept going, sprinting backward. "One or two questions, that's all, then we'd leave. See if your mom will let you, okay?"

"I'll . . . try," she said in a small voice.

The hall had emptied out. I turned to dash the last few yards and leap up the familiar steps to the south wing hall, but I miscalculated; the steps were already under me. I stumbled back, trying to catch a step with my heel, but my backpack was weighing me down. I spun to face the steps. The weight of the pack shifted as my feet tried to claim a foothold. I slipped down a step. Another try, another miss. I pitched forward, sprawled the length of the steps. My backpack went flying over my head, pulling my face down. My forehead hit tile with a *thunk*.

Spread-eagle on the stairs, like a facedown, half-baked gingerbread man, I hoped for all I was worth that Reece had gone on to her class. I wouldn't have cared if half the school spilled into the hallway for the pleasure of seeing me fall, as long as Reece hadn't seen it.

Crumpled, forehead bruised, and wearing my backpack practically on my head, I slithered back down the hard metal edges, turning as I went until I was back where I'd started. I looked down the hall and there she stood, all by herself at the other end, clutching at her waist, giggling until her shoulders shook.

"Hey, Elijah Creek—" she paused to gasp air, "hey (more giggles), I have a pair of crutches you can rent. Cheap."

The twins were in bed. I was supposed to be. I crept downstairs past the Christmas tree and the button-eyed bears in the living room. My purpose was to beg Mom and Dad to ease off just a teeny bit more on my grounding so I could visit Dowland one last time. If I pulled if off, I'd try to weasel another un-grounding for a powwow. Then I'd never ask for another favor as long as I lived.

"Mom? Dad?" I padded barefoot into the kitchen. "There's something I want to ask . . . Mr. Dowland about."

Mom looked up from a pile of coupons. "The police are questioning him, hon. You don't need to."

"They did already, Mom. He claims he knows nothing. But he knows." I sat at the table with them.

"What does he know, dear?" She went back to sorting and clipping.

"Who the victims were. And I think I know too."

Dad's eyes came off the paper and landed on me.

"Who do you think it is?" he asked warily.

"I'm not positive, but I think I know how to get it out of him."

"How?" Dad asked. He put the paper down.

"Can I talk to him first and give you an answer when I know for sure?"

"He's unstable, Elijah. You said so yourself. After what happened with that dog . . . no, Elijah, I won't have you taking that risk." He went back to his paper, as if that settled it.

"Then you come with me, Dad."

Mom looked up. "Why not let the police—"

"Because this involves the armor!" I pleaded.

He gave me a weary look. "Elijah . . ."

"You've got to trust me on this, Dad."

"No, son, *you* need to trust *me*."

"Reece is asking her mom right now. Either you or Mrs. Elliston could take us there." The more I pictured it in my mind, the clearer it got. "See, you can wait in the car where he can see you, so he doesn't try anything. Simple and safe!"

I knew he didn't understand. How do you explain to your dad that maybe, just maybe, God has called you to put on his belt of truth and then go do something, like fight some kind of war, but you don't know yet what kind of war?

"I know you're worried," I said. "I'm not all that keen on going to his house either. But—" I got up to raid the cookie jar. "I have to."

They studied me. I shrugged. "That's all, I just do. I have to know the truth. I uncovered this mystery, and I want a part in solving it."

"We love you, Elijah," Mom said. "We don't want you hurt."

"I know." I went to the fridge to get some chocolate milk.

Dad said, "His dog is gone, but the danger is not over."

"Don't think I haven't worried about it," I said.

The room got quiet. Mom frowned at her coupons, like she wasn't listening.

I asked a question, knowing it had no sure answer. "See, because I've been wondering . . . when a good man goes bad, just *how* bad does he go?"

Mom and Dad looked at each other.

"For reasons unknown I've been dragged into a death I had nothing to do with. And if Reece and I are the only ones who can get to the bottom of it, shouldn't we try?"

Mom shook her head and stuffed the coupons in an envelope. "It's between you two men. You'll have to call Reece's mother, Russ. Whatever you decide." She kept shaking her head and blinking and making a frustrated sound in her throat, like she was going to short-circuit.

It was the first time she'd ever called me a man.

Chapter 19

DAD stopped the car across the street from 26 Jewett Avenue in Newpoint and turned to me, worried. "I think I should go in with you." He glanced at Reece in the back seat.

I felt like we'd get more out of Mr. Dowland if it were just Reece and me and told Dad as much.

"No more than five minutes," he said, "or I'll be coming in."

We walked cautiously up to the door, Reece wincing with each step. She'd been doing well since finding the belt, but today was stressful. When we got to the door, I turned and gave Dad the thumbs-up.

Reece looked at me. "Ready?"

"As I'll ever be."

She smiled bravely at me and knocked on the door. "Who starts?"

"I will."

She set her chin, clamped her eyes shut for a second, and breathed in slowly.

"Praying?" I asked.

"Yep. The truth will set you free."

The window curtain moved.

"He sees us," I said.

Nothing happened. She knocked again. After a long moment, we heard locks and bolts moving. The door opened. I'd warned Reece ahead of time that Dowland was scary in a pitiful way. She was ready for him with a beaming smile.

"Hi, Mr. Dowland," I said. "This is Reece. She's the one I told you about before."

His eyes shifted between the two of us.

She kept her smile. "It's nice to meet you, Mr. Dowland. May we talk with you for a minute?"

"Not the best time," he said flatly.

"We won't stay long. We just wanted to know if we were able to do what you wanted us to?"

He kept sizing us up, as if we were kids selling vacuum cleaners door-to-door. "What'd that be?" he finally asked.

She leaned in. "I wish we could have kept the whole thing quieter. We didn't understand that part until it was too late. We'll do better next time."

His eyes narrowed. "I don't know what you're talking about."

"We want to help, piece by piece, so they can all rest in peace."

Her words registered.

"Come in," he said grudgingly, "but you can't stay long."

The living room was painted an icy blue and was cramped with fifty-year-old furniture and dusty stacks of magazines and newspapers. It seemed to me Dowland's whole world was stuck in the past while his body had skipped ahead a couple of decades. I noted the familiar green-gray flannel shirt and dry, cracked face—the face of Telanoo. I wondered if that's what happens to a person or a piece of land that belongs to no one: it just dries up and dies.

Dowland closed the door behind us and looked around as if he'd lost something. Reece and I sat on a couch covered in a faded navy blanket. There were no family pictures. I noticed a stale smell of dog.

"The clue was excellent, sir," Reece said. "We found her for you. We found them both. Now they can rest in peace." She gulped back her nerves. "It was a very good thing you did."

"Why'd you come?" He was already drifting toward outer space.

She said, "We thought you might tell us more, so . . . so, um . . . we could help you again."

"I don't need help."

Reece was at a loss. She shot a look at me.

I threw out a cheerful, "Well, we know about Theobald— and the baby."

Mistake number one.

Whatever was caged in his mind broke loose. His face went chalky, his thin lips lost all color. He brought up bony fists. "Why, you little meddling brats!!"

I knew he was no Mr. Personality, but that was way out of line.

I sat tall. "Excuse me, but don't say that about my friend."

"Get out!"

I'd heard that before. "Reece, let's go." I helped her up. We headed for the door. I wanted more information, but his reaction showed that we'd hit on the truth. I turned. "Sir, I thought I should explain about your dog. I'm sorry about killing him, but he attacked us. I had no choice."

On the one hand I wasn't sorry at all. Then I remembered how Reece had cried in the hallway over the mess Mr. Dowland had gotten himself into. From the look of things, he might never get out. I felt bad for him, trapped in a cold, smelly house.

He looked around for Salem, then back at us as if trying to make the connection. A word slipped out of his mouth that I didn't catch.

I decided to give it one more try. "Mr. Dowland, if your daughter's death was an accident, why didn't you tell someone?"

"They should have helped you," Reece jumped in.

He tried to focus.

"The church should have helped you," she repeated.

His face went into a kind of landslide. His head drooped. "No one stood by me. No one." He croaked in an evil voice, "They owed me for all I did. They *owed me!* Shame on them all!"

We eased open the door. In spite of how he'd acted, Reece turned to him kindly one last time, "'Piece by piece they *will* rest in peace.' It will be all right, Mr. Dowland. I'll pray for that."

His head turned mechanically in our direction. In a hateful tone he sneered, "Hell and damnation to all who bring trouble on the house of God!"

I took Reece's hand. "Well, thank you. If you have any more pieces we can help you with, just feel free to let us know, anytime—"

She elbowed me hard in the ribs.

Big mistake number two. I was so antsy about getting the next piece of armor, I'd spewed out an open invitation for Dowland to just show up at my door. Night or day.

We stepped outside. I turned back, "But call first, okay? Call *first*."

He slammed the door.

We got in the car and punched the locks down.

"You okay, kids?" Dad asked.

"That was strange," Reece said calmly.

I turned toward the back seat. "Hey, Reece, what did he mumble when I mentioned his dog?"

Her face was full of sadness. "He said, 'Jerusalem.' I think it was his dog's real name, Elijah. Maybe he didn't name his dog for a witch town after all. *Jerusalem* means 'city of peace.'"

I was speechless. A dog like that named City of Peace?

We thought about it as Dad fired up the engine. Telanoo and Dowland and Salem all may have started out good, but somehow had turned evil. *Why?*

Dad headed out of Newpoint without a word, glancing

sideways at me, then at Reece in the rearview mirror. Halfway to Magdeline, he said, "You have to tell the police how Mr. Dowland acted and what he said. Let's stop by the city building."

Officer Taylor was called in from patrol. He took us to a small, plain room to hear us out. It was intimidating to sit there and tell the strange unvarnished truth as best I knew it, but I told him what I believed. Some thirty-odd years ago Stan Dowland and the Theobalds had gone for each other's jugulars over a land dispute, and that we believed Dowland had hidden his daughter away from the younger Theobald and the rest of the town to hide his embarrassment about a baby.

Officer Taylor watched me like a hawk.

Reece gave her ideas, that maybe the girl didn't know the well was there and fell in accidentally. Or maybe her boyfriend found out she was hiding and went to the old house. Maybe she tried to run and hide to save her dad's reputation. Reece and I didn't want to think that girl had killed herself. And as much as we didn't trust Dowland, we couldn't believe he'd push his own daughter down a well.

It was almost dark when we headed home. On the way to Reece's apartment, I turned to the back seat to tell her thanks for coming. She looked especially small all by herself back there. Her eyes were closed and she was smiling.

"You look like the canary who just ate the cat," I joked.

Her eyes drifted open and fixed on me. In an eerie, other-worldly voice she said, "Piece by piece."

Chills went down my spine. I didn't know what to make of it. But that night I dreamed she was the ghost of Dowland's daughter, coming back to settle the score.

Chapter 20

WHILE setting up the stage for the Christmas Village program, I saw just how loopy my life had become. I was a grounded outdoorsman; a police informant by day, baby-sitter by night; the keeper of the armor of God without one lousy piece of it in my possession. And my two best friends were running around in pointy green hats and leotards. My situation had reached freak-show weird.

Elementary shoppers swarmed through a pint-size version of Magdeline's business district. Robbie and Reece stood behind tables of merchandise, making change for the little customers who couldn't add. The twins got Dad a mug that said World's Best Dad in Old English lettering and a nice pen in a velvet box. I recommended a butterfly pin for Mom. We got Grandma Creek doilies and homemade jam.

The twins made me leave while Robbie helped them pick out my gift. There wasn't much I was interested in. But to avoid getting stuck with a plastic dump truck or a bright blue death noose—formally called a youth tie—I signaled Robbie that I liked a yellow flashlight with black trim. It had two settings—wide and narrow beam—and a metal ring to attach it to a belt or backpack.

I hadn't planned on buying anything there, but Reece was admiring a silver cross necklace, so I snuck it out at the last minute and slipped the money to Robbie. I bought another type of necklace with beads for Mei so their gifts would be sort of the same. The Swiss army knives were pretty nice. I bought one each for Robbie and Skid. All in all, I didn't do half bad.

Things were winding down by lunchtime. Mom had recruited Mrs. Aizawa to bring refreshments. When Mei came in carrying trays of goodies, I saw a chance for the five of us to squeeze in a quick powwow. I ran out to the pay phone in the hall and called Skid.

"Hey, we're at school. We'll be closing down the Christmas Village soon. I'm still grounded, but right now I'm on neutral turf. Could you get here for a powwow?" I glanced out the side door. The day was cold, sunny, and dry: good conditions for a skateboarder. "You could be here in a few minutes on your board."

"Be there pronto, Tonto," he said, and hung up.

I wandered to the window of the band room. In less than five, Skid swooped in like a hawk, smooth as silk, his eyes focused on the blacktop and nothing else, hair blowing like feathers. In one liquid motion he came to a stop at the bottom of the steps, flipping the board precisely into his outstretched hand.

Down to a science, I said to myself, jealous and awed.

Skid helped us disassemble the village storefronts, haul them to the commons, and stash them backstage. I told Mom I'd be hanging with my friends until she was ready to go. With the cleanup ruckus going on in the main area, we were able to dissolve into the background. We found chairs and made a tight circle behind the rear curtains at the back of the stage.

Reece and I updated everyone about our meetings with Dowland and Officer Taylor.

Mei could hardly believe any of it. "You went to Mr. Dowland!? *Baka mitai!*"

"*Baka*-what?" Robbie asked.

"That seems crazy!" she said. "Your father took you to the police station to tell the story? *Sugoi!* This is strange to me."

"*Sugoi* ditto!" Robbie said, throwing his head back and scrunching his eyes shut. "Dowland *and* Taylor!"

Skid updated us on his news: "I called the Stallards like you wanted, Creek. I told them about the trouble down here. They're willing to meet with our parents to smooth things out, but they'll need to squeeze us in before they head to Bethlehem for Christmas."

Reece gasped. "Bethlehem? As in the *real* Bethlehem? The birthplace of Jesus?"

Skid nodded.

"Wow . . . how awesome is that?!" she breathed.

"Are they bringing the belt of truth?" I asked.

"I guess so. They didn't say," Skid answered.

"But it's *ours!*" Eight eyes glared at me. I didn't mean to bark, but that's how it came out. "Well, it *is,* and I say we get it back. Skid, if you wouldn't mind, remind them just so there's no mess up."

"Sure," he said.

"Okay, that's taken care of. On to new business: we should be looking for the next piece of the treasure," I said. "I'm working on a map of the camp. If we talk through all the clues, we may come up with something. One thing's for sure, we're not going to get any more information out of Dowland about the treasure or the murder or anything else."

At that very moment my Indian senses kicked in. Someone was standing on the other side of the curtain. I put my finger to my lips. Quickly I stood and walked cat-quiet toward the curtain. With one arm I swept it back.

"Nori! Stacy!" I lashed out. "What are you doing sneaking around like that? We're having a private conversation."

"Mommy said it's time to go," announced Stacy, her mischievous smile an exact copy of her sister's. They'd been listening in.

The next Monday the gym filled up as Robbie and I made our way in for the school Christmas concert. Skid waved us up to the top bleacher.

There he was, cool as a cucumber, one foot propped on the bleacher in front of him, his chin resting on his fist. His eyes roamed over the crowd. I hoped he was keeping a lookout for Miranda.

"I've been back to Florence's," he said after a minute.

"By yourself?" Robbie asked.

Skid's head rotated toward us. "I sat with the Romeos this

time, the same three as before: Obie, Walter, and Charlie. Turns out Walter, the quiet one, is related to the Theobalds. That day we talked to them, he was just taking it all in."

"And?"

"Brace yourself, boys. The whole thing's blown open around town and Bruce Theobald's fighting mad."

"Mad at who?" I asked.

He eyed me with an air of mystery, giving me a minute to figure it out.

I gulped. "Walter told him about *us?*"

Skid nodded. "Said he didn't mean any harm, but felt 'beholden to the family.' When Theobald had to fess up to his family why the police questioned him, his wife pitched a fit and moved out."

"That's just great!" I griped. "Now both suspects in the murder hate us!"

The band started tuning up.

Looking on the bright side for a change, Robbie said, "What are you getting in a lather over? Theobald doesn't know us."

"He has our first names," I said. "How many Elijahs are there in Magdeline? How many teenage boys eating grits and bacon at Florence's at the crack of dawn?"

"There's another Robbie," my cousin said hopefully.

"Robbie *Cardosi?!*" I yelled. "He's seven years old, for crying out loud!" I'd just about had it with him weaseling out of responsibility, thinking he could be part of a quest with no risk involved. I went off like a siren, "But there's only *one Robbie WINGATE!*"

People turned and stared. Robbie slumped down. I'd made my point.

When I cooled off, I said to Skid, "So Bruce Theobald's mad, so what? No skin off my nose."

The choir made its way to risers set up on the floor. Mei and Reece came into the gym. I waved. Reece waved back, but took a seat with some friends down front so she wouldn't have to climb the steps.

I lowered my voice, "Skid, did you learn anything about Theobald from the Romeos?" As if I had to ask. Skid probably had everything from his genealogy to his shirt size.

"The bad news keeps coming," he said calmly. "He's a bulldozer operator."

Robbie groaned, "Heavy machinery! He's going to squash us like bugs."

Skid went on. "Theobald lives on High Street. He's married, has four kids, all grown; but two boys still live at home."

"High Street, huh?" I thought out loud. "I know where that is."

Skid leaned over and lowered his voice. "This'll interest you. The Romeos didn't seem all that surprised about the discovery of the remains, or that it might be Dowland's daughter."

I stared at him.

"Odd, isn't it?" he said. "Another thing, when Kate Dowland left town all those years ago, people suspected that her family was lying about the reason. Dowland told people she was going to Ireland as an exchange student. Dowland even had people write letters to her, which he supposedly mailed to Ireland. And get this: Theobald was a big name around town back then. You see what I'm saying? The family had money, influence."

I thought about that. "Behind Dowland's back the church was siding with people high on the social ladder?"

Robbie looked puzzled. "Wow. I didn't know Magdeline *had* a social ladder.

Skid said, "According to the Romeos, the church let him sink like a rock."

Robbie replied, "But *he* lied to everyone about his daughter, and he was a minister! They're not supposed to lie."

"No one is *supposed* to lie," Skid said.

Chapter 21

WITH the Christmas Village behind us and Mom back on the home front, I got un-grounded. First thing, I took my bike out for a spin down Main Street. People smiled and waved, but after what Skid had said, I wasn't sure I trusted them. On the way home I made a side trip to High Street. I wanted a peek at the place where the old boyfriend lived.

You'd think High Street would be high, but it wasn't. Sure, the High Street bridge arched up over the railroad tracks. But from there it was downhill all the way. The paved street broke down into potholes and gravel, then bottomed out into a gully of rubble. High Street had only about ten small houses jammed together. *They should have named it Down-and-Out Street.* I began to wonder if nothing in Magdeline was as it seemed.

I coasted to the end of the pavement, turned around, and pumped back up the hill a few yards, stopping just shy of the bridge. There was nowhere to go without being flat-out conspicuous. I pretended to mess with the handlebars and snuck a look down the hill.

The Theobalds' driveway was a stretch of dirt crowded with old cars. The squat little house, painted white but fading to a yellowish gray, seemed way too small for a big family. To my shock, Bruce himself stepped outside. I'd counted on him being at work, but there he was, a husky man in gray work pants and a dirty undershirt. His size dwarfed the covered porch where he stood taking a smoke. As I turned my bike to make a quick escape, my right foot slipped off the pedal and went under the bike. I almost went down. I recovered quick as I could, but the mishap drew his attention.

"Hey, you, kid!" he yelled after me, but I kept going. All the way home I thought about how the mighty Theobalds had sunk all the way down to High Street. Maybe what happened those years ago had somehow tipped over Magdeline's social ladder. Or maybe it was the curse of the armor of God.

Because Robbie's house was, as Aunt Grace put it, "in transition," and because Reece and her mom lived in a small apartment, and because the Skidmore condo was "too vertical" for big parties, Mom arranged for the families to meet the Stallards at our house.

Everyone brought food. And Grandma Creek came.

My grandma is tall and round and healthy for an old person. Her hair is almost all white, and her face is friendly. She likes her name. "It's the most versatile of all names," she says. "I can be Elizabeth or Eliza or Betty or Beth or Betts or Liz or Lizzy. Take your pick." She gets a charge out of telling old stories and people doing embarrassing things, like their pants ripping or laughing so hard they wet themselves. And she loves it when people fall down. I know this from personal experience.

The Stallards showed up on the dot at 7:00. This time they came dressed like professors, wearing dark suits. Dr. Eloise had on fur-lined boots fit for a Canadian winter, though there wasn't a flake of snow outside. Dr. Dale carried his ragtag briefcase.

Mr. Aizawa was in a suit too, stiff and formal. His thick hair and bushy eyebrows made him look stern. Mrs. Aizawa brought a humongous tray of Japanese goodies, and Aunt Grace snagged her right away about recipes for the future Wingate Bed and Breakfast and Tea Room. Mrs. Aizawa smiled and nodded at everything Aunt Grace said, but Mei shook her head at us—her mom wasn't catching much of it.

I'd met Mrs. Elliston a couple of times before. She was small and blond like Reece. She gave all us kids little hugs and told us, "Merry Christmas," and asked how we were doing. "You all right, Elijah?" She tipped her head at me. I could tell she meant it; her smile was a little worried.

"I'm okay," I said.

Mei and Reece ate with the twins at the breakfast table and kept them occupied. The adults ate in the dining room. We guys took trays into the family room and ate beside the fire. Everybody was chitchatting and friendly through the meal, but tension was in the air—except when Grandma told one of her stories. Then there was lots of chuckling.

During dessert, while everyone sat around drinking coffee, Dad finally brought up the subject of the armor. Skid,

Robbie, and I weaved our way into the corner of the dining room to be on the fringes of the conversation. The girls were opposite us in the other doorway, listening. Grandma brought in a rocking chair and sat.

Dad didn't pull any punches. He was polite but "expressed his displeasure" about the Stallards telling us kids to keep the treasure hunt a secret from our parents.

Dr. Eloise's thin fingers came to her mouth. "Oh, dear. We've been terrible. Oh, Dale, haven't we been just awful?"

"Mr. Creek—" Dr. Dale began.

"Please call me Russ," Dad said.

"Russ—and all of you—we do apologize. We meant no harm or disrespect whatsoever. We simply didn't think. Our Hester is grown now, but what an independent girl she was at that age."

Dr. Eloise said, "How upset you must be with us! How can we redeem ourselves?" She turned to the Skidmores. "This is no excuse, of course, but your lovely Marcus was so mature when he visited Dale. My husband was terribly impressed with his interest in archaeology at the museum."

I leaned over to Skid and snickered, "You do look sooo *lovely* tonight, Marcus."

He whispered back through clenched teeth, "Just wait, Creek." He nodded. "That one's going to cost you."

Dr. Eloise went on. "*All* your children are so delightfully intelligent and resourceful."

"Maybe a little too resourceful," said Dad, glancing at me.

Dr. Dale stood and adjusted his glasses. "Let me begin by saying that we are scientists, searching for truth. In defense of our actions, we do have legitimate reasons for confiding in the children." He cleared his throat. "Many of the greatest prophets and leaders of the faith began quite young with special callings: David who slew Goliath, the boy Samuel, young Jeremiah, and Daniel. Many great prophets heard from God in their youth. 'Blessed are the pure in heart, for they will see God.'"

"I'm sorry, but I don't understand what you are saying," Mom said warily.

"Don't misunderstand us, please," Dr. Dale went on. "We are not saying that your children are going to become prophets or lamas or any such thing. No, no," he chuckled.

Robbie nudged me and moved his neck like a llama.

"Not that kind of llama," I whispered.

He made a face and whispered back, "I know!"

"The Word of God is complete. Let's be clear on that point," Dr. Dale continued. "But its messages still speak truth to us in new ways. And sometimes the clearest eye," he nodded toward me, "can see the deepest. The Scriptures are very deep."

Dr. Eloise chirped, "Deeeeep, deepdeepdeepdeep."

Robbie stifled a snort and stashed himself in the corner.

"And so very alive," she added.

"Alive," Dad said thoughtfully. "In what way?"

"In every way: active—working!" Her face tilted up, her

arms went out like she was welcoming a crowd. "Oh, how can you fathom its depths? How can you drink an ocean?"

Dr. Dale nudged her. "One gulp at a time." They grinned at each other.

I didn't get it. By the look on the other parents' faces, they didn't either. All except Mrs. Elliston. She was smiling.

Dr. Dale went on, "Our belief is that if children are specifically called by God for a task, they must be free to obey—within the bounds of safety, of course. We adults with our agendas should not hinder their calling to suit our purposes."

Dad said, "So, if I am understanding you correctly, you're telling us that this relic they found is some kind of sign that they've been . . . chosen by God?!"

For some reason I piped up. "Yeah, Dad. That's what they're saying."

Everyone looked at me as if I'd grown two heads.

"Well, not exactly, Elijah," Dr. Dale corrected. "If you are called, you won't need a relic to prove it. But the fact that you have found something of this nature begs the question, now doesn't it?"

"This armor is the stuff of myth," Dr. Eloise interrupted excitedly, "now brought into the realm of history."

"An artifact of great controversy," Dr. Dale said.

I spoke up again. "Mr. Dowland found the armor first. Does that mean *he* was called by God?"

"Perhaps," Dr. Eloise said.

"But terrible things happened to him," I said.

The doctors eyed each other mysteriously. Dr. Dale said, "True. But were they troubles of his own making or from outside forces? How did he respond to the armor's message?"

The whole room got quiet except for the creak of Grandma's rocker. Again I spoke up. "I think I've been chosen. Reece thinks so too."

Mom leaned over to Dad and said under her breath, "They've been brainwashed, Russ."

I picked up on that and said, "I'm fine, Mom."

She blushed. "But you've been hiding things from us, Elijah. I wouldn't call that fine—thinking you're on a secret mission, that you've uncovered this . . . this thing from God?!"

"Yeah, I lied to you," I said. "And it was wrong. But that was before; I get it now."

The others had been strangely quiet, like they didn't know what to ask. Mom asked, "Carlotta, what do you say about this?"

Mrs. Skidmore turned to the Stallards. "Well . . . if we're getting it all out on the table, I don't really know you that well. You are well-credentialed archaeologists. That's all I know."

Mr. Skidmore, who had a presence that would make anybody stand down, chuckled. "No offense, Stallards, but I had you checked out through military intelligence. You're not terrorists, kidnappers, or smugglers," he looked at the parents, "if that helps."

What a slam! I thought. *Skid's parents have put them on the spot.*

But Dr. Eloise said excitedly, "Excellent, Mr. Skidmore. If we should need to take the children overseas, we already have clearance."

"Wait a minute. Overseas?" Mom cut in.

"Not immediately, perhaps much later. There's preliminary research to be done, the other pieces to find, the question of Ireland where Mr. Dowland initially found the relic . . ."

"Next year, perhaps," said Dr. Dale soothingly, "or the year after. It's up to the children to find the other pieces first. And we are here only to assist."

You could have knocked me over with a feather. Me? Overseas? At first I figured they were just throwing out this crazy stuff, so whatever they *really* wanted us to do would seem tame by comparison, and our parents would be relieved and say yes. Then I snuck a look at Skid. His eyes slid to me, one eyebrow shot up, and he grinned. "Welcome to the world, Creek."

It was clear no one knew how to take the Stallards. Honestly, they were a little left of center.

Tense and red-faced, Uncle Dorian spoke up. "Dr. Stallard, you were talking about us adults having our agendas. What's in it for *you?* Let's hear *your* agenda!!"

The room got quiet again.

As if right on cue, Grandma let out the longest, juiciest, most cavernous belch you ever heard. I'm not kidding, if I hadn't heard it come from her own mouth, I would have bet a camel had snuck into the dining room and let fly.

It was hard to get everyone's reactions, I was so busy trying to control myself. But stern Mr. Aizawa's face finally cracked into a big smile, and his wife said something about the effects of onions. Grandma said, "Oh, dear me!" as she got up with a snicker and a groan and went into the kitchen. Reece's mouth was frozen in a big *O*. The adults tried to pass it off, biting their lips, pretending it hadn't happened. But Robbie curled himself into the corner again, sank to the floor, and snorted his lungs out.

Chapter 22

THAT belch was Heaven-sent. Everyone relaxed and had another round of coffee and dessert. The crowd regrouped around the kitchen counter. Dr. Dale stood at the end in lecture mode and summed up: "As I stated before, our agenda is truth. The armor of God is a spiritual reality, that much we know. But the possibility that a physical representation of that truth has worked its way through the centuries, well! . . ."

I was waiting for an answer that would keep the tension from building again, but the Stallards just stood there with distant, happy smiles.

Uncle Dorian said gruffly, "So all you want out of the deal is . . . truth?"

"No small thing, Mr. Wingate. No small thing," said Dr. Dale.

Aunt Grace touched her husband's arm and said softly, "I could go along to Ireland, dear—do some shopping for the business."

"Can we see the belt?" I asked.

"Certainly."

The moms cleared the dining room table. The Stallards brought out a linen packet, unwrapped it, and spread the belt on the table. To the side of it they opened up the old blanket holding the piece of chain mail.

The grown-ups studied the belt.

"What we discuss here should not leave this house," said Dr. Dale seriously. "I am only trying to spare you trouble."

"What kind of trouble?" Mom asked.

"Could be anything, anytime," Dr. Eloise said. "Publicity hounds, antiquity pirates—or nothing at all. Such is the nature of our work. Now," she pressed her hands together, "we need to tell the children what we have discovered. Elijah, shall we sit here for our little discussion? Any of you parents are welcome to listen in, if you don't trust us."

"Here in the dining room will be fine," Mom said with a weak smile.

"First our little scrap of mail." Dr. Eloise flipped through her Bible. "We looked up every 22:25 in the whole Bible, and we think we have the answer. Job 22:25 says, 'Then the Almighty will be your gold, the choicest silver for you.'" She put the Bible down and smiled. "The Hebrew word for gold here is *betser* and refers to metal in a crude state, or 'dug out,' as in a treasure uncovered. What is fascinating is that the root word also carries the idea of defense. It may be translated gold, or treasure, or defense. And it looks like you children have found all three!"

"We believe this scrap of gold mail is telling you that God himself will be your treasure and your defense."

"Cool," said Skid.

Dr. Eloise added. "The engraver—whoever he was—had a deep understanding of spiritual warfare."

Some of the parents were hovering over our shoulders. Before any of them could flip out, Reece's mom said, "Let's go sit by the fire in the other room. I'll explain what she means by that."

Dr. Eloise smiled at me. "Are we correct that the mail was buried with the helmet of salvation and arm of fellowship, but is not a part of either?"

"As far as we could tell," Robbie said.

"This piece did not fit anywhere," Mei agreed.

"We're still speculating why, but perhaps its message boils down to this: fellowship with each other and with the Almighty is a powerful defense when trouble comes." She held the piece to the light. The two-inch square gleamed and glittered. "It's quite remarkable that this tiny piece was not lost."

"Mei found it stuck in the bottom of the sack," Reece said.

The Stallards congratulated her.

"Let's go on to the belt," Dr. Dale said. "The leather is relatively new, a few centuries old, the tapestry a few centuries older still. Curious, isn't it, that the tapestry is older than the leather it's applied to?"

"How can that be?" Mei asked.

"We're not sure yet. But the tapestry is Coptic, from northern Africa. The metal pieces strung along the back are decorative, but also may have some use in battle. Now, let's look at the buckle. This design here is a Hebrew word; the letters from right to left are pronounced: *awlef, mame, noon*. The word is *omen*. It means 'truth,' 'faithfulness,' and is virtually the same word as *amen*. When we say amen at the end of a prayer, we are stating, 'May it be true!'"

"So it does say truth!" Reece exclaimed. "I knew it would!"

Dr. Eloise nodded. "It was hidden in plain sight. The truth often does that."

"Now this is where it gets interesting," said Dr. Dale. "The first recorded use of the word *omen* in English, meaning 'portent of doom,' was around 1582. And the age of the metal on which the Hebrew word *omen* is engraved dates from about that time, or perhaps from the early Middle Ages. But the workmanship is quite primitive. Therefore we can't know if the word *omen* conveys truth or doom."

"Or both!" said Robbie.

"Could be," Dr. Dale said. "Our observation about the belt is that it appears quite . . . ageless. It can't be assigned to any single era of time. The tapestry outlasted the leather it was first sewn on, and new leather obviously was acquired to keep the belt intact. The word *omen* means two kinds of truth in two languages from two epochs of time. Quite extraordinary!"

"Quite mysterious," added his wife. "The belt is not eternal, of course, but it certainly hints at eternity, don't you think?"

We sat there, not sure what to make of it.

"Where did the armor come from in the first place?" I asked.

"To answer that we have to go back to the first century A.D. when the apostle Paul was a prisoner in Rome," said Dr. Dale. "Armored soldiers guarded him constantly. He wrote a letter to the Ephesians, a suspicious people who feared the power of gods, demons, and even stars. Paul used the illustration of armor as protection from such worthless ideas. Until Marcus handed us that first piece of mail, we'd only heard legends of an actual suit of armor which carried in it the spiritual power of the Scriptures.

"But why is it here in sleepy old Magdeline?" said Robbie. "Why now? Why us?"

The two doctors of archaeology blinked at each other in Morse code or something.

"Shall I, my dear?" Dr. Dale asked.

"You may," she answered.

He rubbed his chin and glared into our faces. You'd have thought he was a principal, and we had just TPed the school yard.

"One of you—" he began accusingly.

Skid said, "Not me, man. I'm innocent!"

"—has been praying. Okay, which one of you was it?" Dr. Dale's eyes rested on Reece. "It was you, wasn't it?"

A shy smile spread across her face. She curled her finger at him. He leaned over, and she whispered something in his ear.

"Ah! I see, I see." He frowned thoughtfully. "Well, little lady, you may have gotten more than you bargained for."

"Fill in the rest of us," I said.

Dr. Dale smiled. "I'll let Reece tell you in her own good time. We have to consider the Day of Evil."

"Day of Evil, oh yeah," I said.

"Ephesians chapter six tells us to put on the whole armor, so when the Day of Evil comes we will be able to stand our ground. Scholars argue whether there is a specific Day of Evil coming."

"I read you that part before," Reece said to us.

"Of *course* there is a Day of Evil," Dr. Eloise said with cheery gruesomeness. "The last days are coming with untold global chaos, the likes of which never have been seen. Whether this verse refers to that time toward the end is not known. But . . ." her finger drilled up into the air, "the discovery of the armor at this point in time could be verrrrry significant. A signal. An omen!"

Dr. Dale calmly said, "Keep in mind, children, *always* keep in mind that this armor is *not* a magic thing that has touched a dead holy man's big hairy toe bone and has special powers, or some ridiculous thing. We are not talking about sorcery! Are we clear on that?" he asked sternly.

"We're clear," I spoke for all of us.

"The power is in the message, not the metal," I said.

The doctors beamed. "Well put, Elijah. Well put!"

"Reece said it first," I confessed.

"Look at what bright children we have here!" Dr. Eloise said.

Dr. Dale folded the belt carefully. "Press on, kids, press on."

I was glad the parents were talking in the other room. What I mean is, talking with Dr. Dale was cool. But his wife—with her Eskimo boots and business suit, grinning and drilling the air with her finger of doom—well, call me nuts, but I had flashes of Hansel and Gretel's run-in with the witch—all sweetness and candy while she's firing up the stove.

While the moms wrapped their leftovers to take home, Dr. Eloise said to Aunt Grace, "We'll be in contact in the case of international travel. All of you," she raised her voice so the dads standing by the fire could hear, "please know that you are welcome to come along. The children are invited to Chicago anytime too. We can visit the archives!"

"Can we keep the piece of blanket?" Robbie asked. "I'm thinking it could be evidence to a crime."

We filled them in on the latest about the Dowland mystery. They were "appalled" and "intrigued."

"The police might need to see the belt too," I said. "I had to tell them we were digging for treasure."

They didn't like the idea, but they didn't give us any flak either.

I called Reece in by the Christmas tree. "Hey, what did your mom tell my parents—about warfare?"

"I don't know, but here. I have something for you." She gave me a narrow box.

"Wait, let me get your present too." I ran up to my room and grabbed her gift, nearly breaking my neck on the way down the stairs. I was glad I'd gone to the trouble to buy her something.

I opened the gift from Reece. My chin dropped. "Wow, Reece, wow! Where'd you get this?"

"Do you know what it is?" she asked.

"Sure I know! It's an Indian eagle-bone whistle! With real feathers and leather and everything. This is so cool."

"Actually they're made from turkey bones now," she said sheepishly. "Eagle bones can't be used, since some eagles are endangered. It's just a replica, but it really works. Do you know what it's used for?"

"Indians use it in powwows."

She nodded. "To call the Great Spirit. When I thought about getting it for you, I wondered if it was a proper thing for playing music to God. I never heard it used in church, but I thought about it and realized that any kind of music is okay if your heart's right. It's okay not to like pipe organs."

I lifted it from its case, wrapped my fingers around it, and blew. It squeaked and hissed. But after a few tries at putting my fingers in different places, a clear sound pierced the air. Mom peeked into the room to see what the noise was.

"It's an Indian whistle, Mom. From Reece. Isn't it the coolest?"

"It's very nice." She smiled and disappeared.

"It's great," I said, quiet and reverent. "It's the best gift."

I don't mind saying Reece was crazy about the cross necklace. She said it was just what she wanted.

Chapter 23

REECE and I sat in the back seat of her mom's car with the belt of truth wrapped in cloth and the piece of blanket in a sack. After the Stallards left, we'd decided it all had to be turned over to the police as soon as possible. The compass was still missing. Robbie swore I put it in my pocket after the dinner at Mei's. I had a vague memory of doing that, and of having it while I worked on the map, but I couldn't find it. Officer Taylor hadn't called for it, but Reece wanted me to tell him anyway. To help me out, Mei made a sketch from memory.

"What do they do with evidence?" Reece asked her mom as we rode along.

"They study it, I suppose, and keep it until a case is solved."

"What if it's never solved?"

Mrs. Elliston was quiet a long time.

Reece asked again, "What if a case is never solved, Mom?"

"Honey, I think they have the right to keep it in storage."

"Forever?!"

"Hold on a minute," I said, a knot in my stomach. "Can we stop the car and think this over? Officer Taylor never called us back. We already know the belt has nothing to do with Kate Dowland's death. The compass might, and the blanket, but not the belt."

Reece stared straight ahead. Her mom kept driving. I knew what the answer was. "But we can't hide the truth . . . I guess." I unwrapped the belt and spent the last few moments of the ride looking at it: the foreign embroidery and metal decorations, the old leather, the pounded metal bars that spelled out *truth* in an ancient language.

"The Ancient Omen," I whispered reverently.

"The oldest truth in the universe," Reece whispered back. "The truth that will set you free."

The wonder of it washed over me like a flood. It was going to kill me to let it go.

Officer Taylor showed us to a back room. "You have something for me?"

I said, "Officer Taylor, we're still looking for the compass. We can't seem to find it."

He studied me hard for a minute.

"We won't give up though. We'll keep looking. And here's a sketch of it. But we have something else."

Reece gave him the piece of blanket, and even though cops are trained to be cool, Officer Taylor was plainly shocked. "Where did this come from?"

"It was with the first piece of armor we found, which Mr. Dowland stole from us. And, by the way," I added, "if you question him and he happens to mention some old helmet, we'd really like to know."

He called over another officer who had the same reaction and took the blanket into another room right away. *Key piece of evidence*, I thought.

Reece said, "It's a piece of baby blanket, isn't it? Robbie thought it might be from that baby who died in the well."

I could tell by his look—she'd hit the nail on the head.

He nodded toward the belt. "Let's see what else you have there." We opened it up. He looked it over curiously. "Hmm."

"It was with the compass, buried on Devil's—I mean, on that hill next to the meadow. It's part of the set of armor that belonged to Old Pilgrim Church," I explained. "If you don't have any use for it, we'd like to keep it. I mean, you could run tests on it for whatever you need."

"We've already received a packet of sophisticated forensic data this morning from a couple from Chicago." He chuckled and shook his head. "The lab analysis even included a chemical breakdown of the type of soil it was buried in."

Reece and I exchanged amazed looks.

"The Stallards?" Reece asked.

"That was the name," he said. "Did you tell them of the connection between these pieces and the remains found in the well?"

"Yes, sir. Was that okay?"

"Yes." He said cautiously, "They were very eager to help us move the case forward." He studied the belt. "Odd looking thing. What do you plan to do with it?"

"Keep it forever," Reece said.

I said casually, "It's just cool. So . . . can we have it back?"

He hesitated before measuring his words: "Kids, I appreciate this. We need to ask a few more questions around town. I'll have to keep it until then. It's procedure."

"Then we can have it back, after the questions? We don't want the blanket or the sketch," I pleaded.

"We'll see. Thanks. You've been good citizens. Tell your folks I said so. You have a good holiday now."

He wrapped the belt and stood. "And when you find that compass, I'd like to have a look at it." Taking the belt, he went down a back hallway, and just like that it was gone.

"Reece, . . ." I got up and walked to the glass door, staring out at a gray day, feeling as cold and empty as I ever had in my life.

"What's wrong?" she asked.

"I never put it on. I put on the helmet and arm piece that night in Telanoo . . . how could I be so dumb!"

She came up beside me.

"We're back to square one," I said. "And if the mystery of the well is never solved, the belt of truth will spend the next hundred years molding in an evidence box in the back room of the Magdeline City Building."

Suddenly, I wanted to forget I'd ever seen the blasted thing. I hated wanting it so much!

"Elijah, you can't doubt yourself. You did a good thing,

you told the truth. Did you see how they reacted over the blanket? It's important to the case! And about the armor—just have faith." She took hold of my arm. "Maybe, just maybe, the armor is supposed to come together all at once, just in time for the Day of Evil!"

She said it in such a sweet, singsongy voice, that the Day of Evil actually didn't sound half bad. You might even say I was halfway looking forward to the Day of Evil if it meant having the whole armor of God strapped to my body.

Chapter 24

ON Christmas Eve we had a Camp Mudjokivi staff party at the lodge, with everyone and their families, a big fire going, and tons of food. Grandma was the life of the party. "You heard about my burp the other night? Mind if I bring it up again?" she joked. But my mind was elsewhere. I bowed out after dinner to go to my room and finish the map. I wanted to find the next piece of the armor in the worst way.

I transferred all I knew to one final map. Working out from Camp Mudj toward Telanoo, I included a rough sketch of Morgan's barn and house and the main road. It wasn't nearly as cute and colorful as Mei would do, but it was pretty accurate. I included little pictures of the important details: Old Pilgrim Church, the graveyard, the Bone Tree in Telanoo, and the ruin where the skeletons were found.

Later that night, the twins padded into my room in jammies and socks while I was finishing the compass rose.

"Whatcha doing?" Nori asked.

"Drawing a map."

They climbed up on the bed beside me.

"What's it of?"

"The camp and stuff."

I pointed out the special places.

"What's that for?" Nori pointed to the compass rose.

"It shows the direction to important places where I've found special things."

"What things?" Stacy asked.

"The dead people," Nori answered.

"We're not talking about that, you hear?" I scolded. "This map is for finding good things."

"Can we help you find the things?" Nori asked.

I said it was too far and too cold, and they said no it wasn't. I said yes it was and if they didn't go to bed, Christmas would never come. They said a few words in their secret language, and I said, "If it's something about me, you better not!" They giggled and left.

I practiced a tune on my Indian whistle until Mom came in to hug me good night.

Somehow after Christmas I got grounded again.

Dad brought me into the living room one evening like before, except the mood wasn't mellow this time.

"There's been more trouble," he said.

I waited.

"I've been told that Stan Dowland and Bruce Theobald claim you've been spreading lies about them."

"Dad, I haven't talked!" I bellowed. "Me and Robbie have been telling each other every day, 'Mum's the word, mum's the word!' Doggone, it's Justin Brill and his gang and the Romeos and the town gossips, all making trouble!"

He sat there studying his hands.

"I'm not lying, Dad," I defended. "The only one I've said anything to at all is Reece, just once in the school hallway with no one else around. And I only told her because I wanted her to go with me to Dowland's!"

He took a deep breath. "Be that as it may . . . your mom and I think it would be best if you stay close to home for the next little while."

It sank in quick. "You're grounding me again? But I didn't do anything!"

"Just for a short while, Elijah. And it's not a grounding."

"How long is a short while?"

"We'll have to see."

"That's not fair, Dad. If people are lying about me, why should *I* be punished?"

"It's not a punishment, son. We're acting on the advice of Officer Taylor."

It was like a punch in the stomach. "Officer Taylor?" The deck was stacking against me. My own parents conspiring with the town cop, the one who had the belt of truth with no obligation to give it back, ever. "What about Robbie and Skid? What about them?"

"It's up to their parents. But apparently Bruce Theobald saw you watching his house by yourself. Is that true?"

"Yes, it's true. I went out on my bike when I got un-grounded—one lousy time! I wanted to see . . . if he looked like a murderer. It's the oldest trick in the book, Dad. Shifting blame, that's all they're doing."

"Apparently Mr. Theobald caught Mr. Dowland poking around his house too, and there were heated words. The police were called in. Theobald claims you and Dowland are working against him. So I don't want you going over there," his voice got firm, "or anywhere unnecessarily."

I jumped to my feet, steaming mad. "That's not fair! Grounded over Christmas break!?"

"You're not listening, Elijah. It's not a grounding. You can have friends over as long as their parents agree."

"Oh, man!" I whined. "Why can't I go to *their* houses?"

"You *can* go places, Elijah, but not alone! I'm asking you to be cautious. Use those Indian skills," he tried to smile. "Keep those eyes and ears open."

He pinched the bridge of his nose and rubbed the crease between his eyebrows. I could see what a strain my troubles had put on him. I propped myself against the wall.

"I didn't mean for any of this to happen, Dad. It was a treasure hunt, that's all."

Lightning and thunder rattled the ramshackle windows of The Castle. A thunderstorm rolled through Ohio, a rare thing in the dead of winter. Robbie, Skid, and I were hanging out in the attic the night before school was to start up again. Aunt Grace and Uncle Dorian had gone to Columbus to return some Christmas gifts they didn't like; we had the place to ourselves. We were down in the kitchen getting a snack when the phone rang.

"Hello?" Robbie answered. He paused for a long minute. "Hello?" His face went slack, as his round eyes drifted to us. "They hung up."

"Probably a wrong number," I said casually, piling up Christmas leftovers.

"But they didn't ask for anyone."

The three of us looked at each other.

Skid shrugged. "People do that sometimes. Change their mind, forget what they called for."

"Or they call to see who's at home," Robbie said eerily.

He ran to the entry and came back in ten seconds, then to the back door. "Locked!"

We took our food to the attic and locked ourselves in. Wind whipped bare branches of a big tree against the house.

"Sounds like bony fingers tapping," Robbie said.

"You have sugar on your chin from those cookies," Skid said to distract him.

"Lay off the Bates Motel garbage," I snapped. I lobbed a croquet ball at Mrs. Bates and knocked off her bleach bottle head, which lifted the mood a little.

Robbie finished his cookies and went to the window to watch the lightning. "Guys, there's a car down there!"

Skid tried to act casual getting to the window. So did I. We crowded around the pane and looked down. A big old sedan sat half hidden behind a row of untrimmed hedges. We couldn't tell the make of it.

"Just a car," Skid said, but he kept his face pressed to the window.

I was ready to suggest that Robbie's neighbors probably were having relatives in for the holidays, when I spotted the tiny fiery tip of a cigarette through the windshield.

"See that? That cigarette?"

"Yeah," Skid said, "I see it."

"Someone's in there," I whispered, and my voice was lost in a crack of thunder.

We flipped off the light and took turns watching the car until Aunt Grace and Uncle Dorian got home at 11:00. Right before they pulled in, the car pulled out.

Chapter 25

AS if our situation wasn't tense enough, Dad got a call from Lafe over at the Mad River Boys Ranch, putting us on alert: two of the boys, D-Day and Leon, had gone home for Christmas but had skipped out on their families. They were on the run, and they might be armed.

Joy to the world.

Mom picked me up after school. She said she needed my help with errands, but really it was so she could keep an eagle eye on me. I mostly tagged along. The last stop was the dry cleaners, and she made me lock the doors while she went to get Dad's suit. She looked back to check on me before she went in, and hurried back.

We had just hauled laundry in the front door when Dad came rushing to meet us.

"Are the girls out there?"

"No," Mom said.

"They didn't run out to meet you?" He looked panicked, but said evenly, "I told them to stay in the house. Mrs. Horstley had to leave early; I had business over at the lodge and said I'd be right back."

Mom flung his cleaned suit over the banister and looked up the steps. "They're probably hiding. Girls!" There was no answer. Then to Dad, "You were supposed to watch them!"

"Girls!" No answer. She and Dad locked eyes. A rush of horror went through me. I shot upstairs and swept the area: every nook and cranny of my room, the linen closet, even under the bathroom sink. (The twins are like mice. They can squeeze into places you wouldn't believe.) "Nori! Stacy! Come out. You're worrying Mom and Dad."

Mom and Dad were yelling at each other, searching and calling. I was scared. "Stacy, don't let Nori get you in trouble again," I announced. "Come out now. You're going to get it! Both of you!"

I ran back down to the kitchen. Mom and Dad had scoured the main floor, but I searched it again.

"Where could they be?" Mom asked.

"It was only ten minutes!" Dad defended. "Twenty at the most. They know to stay—" His eyes fell on a piece of paper by the phone. He snatched it up. His face went white. "It's a note from Nori. It says: 'A man called.'"

"Oh no," I muttered. They shot looks at me.

"Elijah . . . what is it? What have you done?!" Mom accused.

"Not me! I didn't do anything! But . . . the other night at Robbie's someone called and hung up, and then there was someone watching the house from a parked car."

"Call the police," Mom told Dad in a flat voice. He grabbed the phone.

I pictured my room again. Something hadn't been right. "Dad, wait a minute. Don't call yet."

I dashed upstairs. Okay . . . everything seemed in place—my books, a pile of clothes. What had I been doing last? The map! It was gone. Suddenly I had an inkling of what may have happened to it . . . and maybe to the broken compass too.

I ran downstairs. "They have my map and the broken compass we've been looking for all this time."

"What do you mean?" Dad cried.

"I made a map of places connected to the armor, and they were asking me about it. Maybe they're just out looking for treasure. Maybe nobody got them after all."

Mom clutched her face in worry. "I still think we should call the police."

"Let me go look," I said.

"You're not going anywhere!" she shot back.

"Mom, if they went into Telanoo with that broken compass, they'll get lost. They don't even know how to use a compass!"

"I'll go," Dad said, grabbing his coat.

Mom looked out the window, worried. "It's freezing out there, Russ! It's already dark!"

"Let me go," I kept on. "I know the trails. I know Telanoo. My hearing's great. I'm fast. I have my new flashlight."

Mom calmed a little and said, "I'm calling the police just for good measure. Because if they're not treasure hunting, where else could they be?"

I hated to bring it up but, "Um . . . well, when the Mad River Boys were here, they did ask questions about the cabins, like who lived there and what was fun to do in town. And they asked if I had sisters."

Mom gasped, and started punching numbers.

Dad said, "I'll check the buildings, Elijah, you take to the trails. If you see anything suspicious—"

"Check the remains of the old church first," I told him. "It was marked on the map. I can take the far cabins on my way into the woods."

I took off on foot down to the lake, knowing I'd make better time without the golf cart. The flashlight's long beam bounced ahead of me on the trail. I stopped and yelled into the wintry dark. "Nori! Stacy!" I listened for a response, but nothing came. I covered more ground, my feet pounding paved road.

There were enough dangers for little kids: the lake, the lagoon, cliffs. What was worse, the most dangerous spots were the very ones I had Xed on the map: the burned out hole that used to be Old Pilgrim Church, the sheer drop-offs of Devil's Cranium . . . and the deadly well. *That's too far into Telanoo. They'd never try it. Even if they went in, they'd never find it.* My eyes watered from the cold.

The well was the least of my worries.

I thought back to Theobald and Dowland. They hated my guts after the mess I'd stirred up around town. Somebody had watched The Castle. Somebody had called my house.

The Tree House Village cabins didn't have locks yet, so I peeked in each one, adjusting my eyes to less and less light. "You in there?" I called again, pausing to listen. "You're in big trouble!"

After that sweep, I zipped between the back cabins. A flicker of light caught the corner of my eye. I skidded to a stop, took a step back into darkness. All my senses went on alert. Was it a reflection of a security light in the window? Or was someone in there, smoking a cigarette?

Running for my life seemed like an excellent idea . . . but what if the twins were in there? *What if some scumbag has my sisters?*

I dropped down below the window and listened for talking or crying. Nothing but quiet clicking high above my head: frozen tree branches tapping in the wind. Creeping to the door, I tried the doorknob ever so slow and quiet. It was locked. But someone was in there; I felt him. I crept around to the other side of the cabin. Sure enough, a screen had been slit.

Go for a surprise attack, I told myself. Bracing myself to kick the door in, I reared back and put all my force behind my foot. *Slam!* It hurt like the dickens, pain reverberating up my leg, but the door didn't budge. I tried again. *Slam!* And again.

"Okay! Okay!" came an angry voice.

The lock clicked, the door opened. I flashed my narrow beam into the disgruntled faces of D-Day and Leon.

"Are my little sisters in there!?" I raged at them.

They looked a little dazed, but not the least bit guilty at getting caught breaking and entering. "You got *sisters?*" D-Day asked innocently.

"Yeah! Are they in there?" The Boys were bigger than me, but I was hot and angry. I pushed past them and scanned the room with my light. "Okay, where are they?"

The guys were stiff as boards, shivering against the cold in thin coats. "We're just hangin', man. We ain't seen nobody."

"Well, my little sisters are lost somewhere and I have to find them . . . and . . . and . . . you're going with me! You've got to get some blood pumping. You want to die of hypothermia?"

They just stood there.

"Let's get moving," I barked. "When we find them, I'll take you back and we'll get warm, but not before. We're in lockdown at Camp Mudj until my sisters are found. So you can stand here and freeze, or help me."

They took off with me, slow and grumbling at first, until Leon mentioned that he had a little sister and he didn't get to see her a whole lot.

We were deep into Owl Woods with no sign of the twins, when I ordered, "We have to split up. Here, you take the flashlight. Circle around. When you get to the creek, follow it back to camp." I handed it over.

"You're going back and leaving us out here!" D-Day asked in a hostile voice.

"I'm going northeast, in there." I pointed into a dark gully that disappeared in the shadows.

His wide eyes peered into Telanoo in disbelief. "You're lying!" he said suspiciously. "You're not going in there!"

"It's okay, I can see in the dark."

"You're lying."

"I'm not. I don't lie . . . anymore."

He shrugged. "Way cool, man. What's up with the night vision?"

"The Indian ways," I explained. "And that flashlight was a Christmas gift from my sisters. It has two beams and a clip. Help me find them and you can have it. I mean that. But try to run off and steal it and . . . all I can say is, I'm working on a case with the police right now, so they know my name, and I'll have them on you like ugly on an ape. You wouldn't want jail time over a lousy flashlight."

The skinnier one, Leon, was so cold he was having trouble breathing. I took off my coat and gave it to him. "Keep moving, you hear? My sisters may be out there and I don't want them freezing."

I was ready to send them into the night, with promises of hot food and a warning about the drop-off cliffs, when I thought about Theobald. "And by the way, there's a big man, a bulldozer operator with short brown hair and a grizzly beard who might be after me. The case I'm working on involved two people he may have killed, so he could be dangerous. Oh, and there's an old guy, skinny and whacko, who's also after me. I killed his dog. If you see anyone like that, run for your life and start screaming. Got it?"

They gaped at me.

Figuring I'd better sweeten the pot all I could, I said, "And one more thing: when we find my sisters, I'll let you both drive the golf cart. Deal?"

They perked up. "Deal."

For being penny-ante criminals themselves, they weren't all that brave, at least not when it counted.

Chapter 26

RUNNING through Telanoo with little more than starlight and a dusting of snow in the creek beds to light the way, I kept telling myself that the ruin and its deadly well were beyond the twins' reach. Then I remembered the straight line I'd drawn from camp, over the Morgan farm to the ruin, as the crow flies. That way would make sense to little kids who knew nothing about trespassing or Black Angus bulls. And if they should be smart enough to compare the compass rose on the map with the broken compass—its arrow glued to east-northeast—it would take them right through the Morgan farm.

Maybe an hour had passed since they'd left. It was fully dark. Pausing to catch my breath—regretting the loss of my coat—I doubled back, then switched directions to due east. I reached the Morgan fence, and I leaped it like I had wings.

Sailing across the smooth, frozen meadows of Morgan's farm, my lungs screamed from the cold air pumping through them.

Lost things floated through my mind: helmet, arm piece, belt, compass, little sisters . . . and all that Dowland had lost: church, daughter, grandchild, wife, everything. I thought of Magdeline losing a nice homey church because of lies and secrets.

I stopped in the middle of Morgan's pasture, wondering where his herd was. "Noriiiiiiiii! Stacyyyyy!" My voice disappeared into the brittle air. I listened for the dread sound of pounding hooves. My eyes blurred from the stinging wind, my heart pounded like a drum in my chest. The ridge was long, sweeping down in front of me toward a wooded gully. Would they have come this way, in the dark? I spun three-sixty, then spun again. *Which way, which way would cold, lost little girls go?*

Maybe they'd already wandered back, or Mom and Dad had found them poking around the old church. Maybe I was killing myself for nothing. And maybe I'd made a huge mistake, sending Leon and D-Day to look for my sisters. I'd gone with my gut though, feeling like there was still some good in them.

The twins would want to go home. But home was hidden by the ridge.

If I were a kidnapper out for vengeance, if I'd lost everyone I loved and wanted someone else to pay the same horrible price, where would I go? Not the well. Too far.

Where would the police look first? Somewhere closer . . .

In the distance was a thin horizon of lights—Magdeline still lit up from Christmas. And between me and Magdeline . . . of course! If I were cold and tired and lost, I'd find a warm place, with warm, dry hay, like the stable in the Christmas story.

Morgan's barn.

I ignored the numbness in my face and limbs and the stitch in my side. Smelling cows and hay as I reached the barn, I cracked open the big door. I listened first, slipped into the blackness and stood with my back against the door. Cows breathed, their big hooves crunching frozen stall muck.

If they're not here, if they're not home, then they're not still wandering Telanoo, I thought with a sick feeling. *Too much time has passed. They've fallen asleep and frozen to death. Or someone has dragged them off, and I'll never see their little matching faces again.*

I didn't want to know the truth.

It took every effort against those feelings of doom to call out, "Nori? Stacy? Are you in here? It's me, Elijah."

Cows chewed and stomped.

"You're in big trouble," I wheezed, my eyes stinging with tears. "Don't hide. I mean it."

A scared little voice called. "'Lijah?"

"Nori?"

"Where are you?" she asked.

"I'm over here. I'll step into the doorway so you can see me. There. Can you see me?"

"Yeah."

"Is Stacy with you?"

"She's asleep."

I followed her voice. "Wake her up, Nori. Don't let her sleep!"

"We got lost," came her voice from a pile of scattered hay bales. A little head appeared.

"Stacy, wake up! Where are you?" I called.

Nori reached out her hand to me. "The compass didn't work."

"Where's Stacy?!" I knelt in the hay beside Nori, frantically feeling for a face or hand.

"Over there. She was too tired."

"Over where?!"

Desperately I felt my way through the bales until my hand found tiny, ice cold fingers, limp on the hay. I scooped her up in my arms. My heart fell. "Oh no . . . Stacy!"

All the ornery things I'd ever thought about my kid sisters came back in a rush. "Come on, wake up, Stace," I choked. I felt so sad and scared and guilty all at the same time, I could hardly breathe. "Gotta go . . . home . . . . Mom and Dad are waiting—"

Then she moved. Her little head turned. "Cold."

My heart leaped. I hugged her big time. "Cold, yeah. I know. Time to go home and get warm."

"'Kay," came the tiny voice.

I got them to Morgan's house and called Mom and Dad. They drove over, and cried and scolded and cried some more.

We were all safe and cozy around the kitchen table when I remembered the Mad River Boys.

"Dad! I found D-Day and Leon! I sent them into Owl Woods to find the girls an hour ago. They should have made it back by now!"

Mom yelled, "Elijah! Have you lost all sense, sending criminals—"

Dad interrupted, "Forget it, hon. We've got to find them."

"I'll get the cart!" I headed for the door.

"Where's your coat?" Mom yelled, then to Dad, "Russ, should we let him?"

"Blankets! I'll need blankets." I flew up the stairs. "And a flashlight."

Mom made that short-circuit sound, but what else could we do? I wouldn't leave my worst enemy lost in the dead of winter in Telanoo.

D-Day and Leon were wandering around off the beaten path, three-fourths frozen. You have to admire their grit; they'd thought they couldn't have a turn with the golf cart if they didn't find the twins, and they weren't giving up. No sooner had I slammed the brake than they started arguing over who'd get to drive first. Leon wouldn't fork over my coat, so I wrapped up in a blanket. Once in sight of the house, I signaled to Mom; she was watching at the window.

We stopped off at our house for hot chocolate, Mom handed out hats and gloves. Then for the next half hour, D-Day, Leon, and I took turns zipping around the frozen lake and through the bare woods, wrapped in blankets like squaws and whooping it up like crazy men. Considering I was a human icicle by then and they were AWOL ex-criminals, we had the best time. I told them if they played it straight, maybe they could grow up to be golf caddies for rich guys at country clubs and drive carts all day. They tried to act like it was a stupid idea, but they were giving it some thought. Dad called Lafe and put in a good word for D-Day and Leon, telling how they helped in the search. I put a good word in too. We made them sound like heroes. Sitting around in my living room, they acted nice. D-Day even told the twins that running off wasn't a good idea. I let them keep my flashlight like I promised.

Chapter 27

WHEN I came down for breakfast the next morning, Mom and Dad were frozen in front of the TV. A reporter was standing beside Dowland's house. A Newpoint cop said Dowland had been dead a few days when his body was discovered.

I dropped down on the couch in shock. "What else? What else can happen?" I asked myself.

The reporter said that new evidence—I figured it was the scrap of baby blanket—had provided another link between Dowland and the remains in the well. They showed a clip of Theobald, who had cleaned himself up for an interview. His side of the story was that Dowland had hidden his daughter Kate and the baby at that old house in the meadow. Theobald said he found out about it—though he didn't say how—and went to see her one night. He'd found the place abandoned. When Dowland claimed he didn't know where they were, Bruce Theobald said he gave up and went on with his life.

Call me nuts, but I wasn't relieved Dowland was gone. All through classes, I kept thinking how he'd broken ties with life and died alone during the holidays while the rest of the world was partying. No matter what he'd done, it was a rotten way to go. I kept waiting to feel okay with it, but that feeling never came. I called Reece after school, and we just hung on the phone without saying much. I knew she was thinking the same thing, but neither of us had the heart to mention it.

You probably know by now that in a crisis, my mind flashes ideas around like heat lightning. I'd already come up with a list of options: Dowland either had been so overcome by bad press and rotten memories that he'd killed himself, or he'd died from the stress, or he'd been done in by the armor of God. "But," I told Reece on the phone, "my mind keeps flickering back to big grizzly Bruce Theobald, standing in front of his shack, calling after me. If he'd loved Kate Dowland and her dad had put a stop to it, if he lost his girl and his child and went into a tailspin all those years ago . . ."

"We may never know," she said quietly.

Have the last clues to the armor of God died with Dowland too?

I tried to keep my mind on other things through the cold days of January, but from the way Mom and Dad talked (sometimes I listened in from the heat vent in the twins' room), they were worrying along the same lines. I wanted to know what the Romeos had to say about all this, but I no longer trusted Walter. I was starting to get why I'd been grounded twice, and why Dad had been so strict with me. This wasn't just the usual parental worry, like when they tell you that any old thing could put an eye out and that all the fun things to do in the world are death traps. They were thinking someone actually might come after me.

When Mom went on errands, she'd leave the twins with Mrs. Horstley at the camp office, and I'd have to go with her. Grandma called and asked if Mom wanted me to come down and stay with her awhile. But Mom said no.

That next Saturday Officer Taylor called us in. The five of us kids went together. On the way I said to Reece, "I have a question."

"Fire away."

"Why didn't God help Mr. Dowland?"

If looks could kill, I'd have been dead meat.

"You have *got* to be kidding!"

I shrunk like a turtle. "I'm just asking, since you're the expert."

"One minute I think you're getting it, then you relapse."

I shrugged. I was clueless.

Then she sighed, laid her head on my shoulder, and whispered, "The truth will set you free."

I was still clueless, but suddenly I wasn't minding so much.

Once at the police station, Officer Taylor came out to the front desk with a sheet of paper in his hand. He thanked us all for our cooperation. "I know this has been rough on you. The blanket you brought in corroborated a journal we found in Mr. Dowland's effects."

"A journal?" I asked.

He nodded. "The blanket gave us a piece of solid evidence.

This case could have gone unsolved for months, or years. The cities of Magdeline and Newpoint thank you."

He shook our hands. Mei bowed. Reece and Robbie beamed. Skid nodded coolly, and I did the same. I gave him the broken compass, in case he needed it. "That journal . . . could we maybe look at it sometime?"

Officer Taylor said, "Well, this won't be in the papers, but you might want to see it. It's an excerpt."

We gathered around an old notebook filled with yellowed paper:

May 10—I confronted Bruce. He denies any knowledge. I think he's lying. There were tire tracks. His? He's taken them somewhere. Kate and Adam, where are you?

May 11—They're still missing. I called Francine. She knows nothing, is worried. Bruce calls me a liar! He accuses me of sending her away, but I think he's hiding something. I'll wait at the house tonight. Where are they??

Nothing was written for the next few days. On the next page was a sad poem. Reece read it out loud:

May 14—I called their names. I called and searched.
The late sun was blood red; I never, ever thought them dead.
But just beyond the fence, a thing beyond all common sense.
A shred of cloth, caught on a bushy thorn
From little Adam's blanket torn.
And from that spot my early shadow fell

Across the open well.
The line is ended, a loss beyond all loss,
Too great a cost, too great a cost.

Reece looked up. Our eyes locked.

I quoted that line from Dowland's story: "'. . . a thing that can't be explained by common sense, a thing no family should ever have to go through.'"

Officer Taylor said, "That piece of blanket was key evidence. Thank you for assisting in the investigation."

I handed over the broken compass. "No prob. So, uh . . . about the belt?"

Officer Taylor gave me a thin smile. "Not yet, I'm afraid. We have to officially close the case, which won't happen until we have gone through all of Mr. Dowland's effects. It may take a few weeks, depending on the case load."

"Sure," I said, "okay. But you could do us a huge favor, if you would, Officer?"

"What would that be?"

"While you're rummaging through his house, if you find anything about armor or things that look like armor, or any paper that mentions armor . . ."

He laughed. "I get your point. Right now, we're trying to find any remaining family members to settle the estate, but if anything turns up, I suppose there's no reason you can't have a look at it. I'll notify the detective."

"And that journal?" I asked.

"We'll see."

Things around Camp Mudj settled back to semi-normal. As for the phone call that came to the house, we never found out who it was. It could have been Theobald; I hadn't let him off the hook yet. But a few days later an aluminum siding salesman called around dinnertime. Mom and Dad were relieved.

The man in the car turned out to be a neighbor, bored with his family, who'd gone out to listen to a game on the radio. On any other night, Skid and Robbie and I probably would have thought nothing of it. But with the storm, and Mrs. Bates sitting there gaping at us, and the Day of Evil supposedly looming ahead, we had every right to expect trouble.

Gossip about the case gradually lost steam. One dramatic newswriter summed up Dowland's tale of woe: "Mad with grief, but unable to retrieve the bodies without exposing his dark secret, Dowland may have covered the well, and simply left them there to be claimed by the earth and the elements. In a journal, he blamed the church for its shallowness, the elder Theobald for his greed, the younger Theobald for unbridled lust, the town for its blind eye. He cursed himself for the lie he'd concocted to cover up the scandal."

The paper said Stan Dowland died of an overdose of heart medication.

Mom read it and cried and hugged me and called me a hero for bringing this sad story to light at such risk. "Finally," she dabbed her eyes, "they can rest in peace."

The hairs on my neck stood up. *Piece by piece they will rest in peace.*

Chapter 28

THE next day, Reece pressed a note into my hand and told me to read it when I was alone. That night in my room, I plopped down on my bed, faceup, unfolded the note, and read:

Dear Elijah,

I asked my mom about what she said about the warfare. She told them about Ephesians 6, like I did with you. She explained that it's not regular war, but supernatural. That it's usually safe, and anyone can do it, even a kid, if he has all the armor.

I know you've been wondering what I whispered to Dr. Dale that night at your house. I'm too shy to tell you in person. Imagine that coming from me—Miss Sarcasm! Well, here it is: I told him that I had prayed for you, starting a couple of years ago. First I just prayed that you'd come to know God better, to grow in spirit and in power, more than anyone else in Magdeline. But soon I knew that my prayer was too small. So I prayed that you'd know him better than anyone in Ohio. Then, I thought, why not the whole country? Or even the whole world?

So that's it. I think God is answering my prayer and something big is coming. I feel it, Elijah. Maybe he had you in mind for his big plan from the start, and I just saw it. If I have brought trouble on you, I'm sorry. Life may not be so easy for you in Magdeline anymore. Whatever happens with the armor, I'm proud to be a part of it.

Your Friend,

Reece

P.S. I'm sorry you got into trouble with your parents, but just think: while you were grounded, you got to talk to the police and solve a mystery, build a mini Magdeline, have breakfast at Florence's (ha), have big, important meetings with important people like the Stallards and the Skidmores, have Christmas with your friends, go on a kayak trip, have a powwow, rescue your sisters, and locate two escaped fugitives. The truth did set you free. Not too shabby!

P.S. again. The next piece is the breastplate of righteousness. So where is it? Huh? Let's get cracking!

She signed off with a smiley face.

I read her note a couple more times, then stashed it in my secret place that the twins don't know about: behind the Indian blanket on my wall. I got the idea from an old movie where they had a safe hidden behind a painting.

I hugged my sisters more, and listened more closely to their secret language, deciding that *lingle* had something to do with getting robbed. I sure didn't want them to lingle any notes from Reece. No way.

Reverently, I took the eagle-bone whistle out of the box and turned it over in my hand, thinking back to what the Stallards had said about fellowship with God being like gold.

I threw on my coat and told Mom I'd be right back. I ran to Great Oak and beyond to The Cedars where my vision quest had taken place weeks ago. I was all set to blow the whistle when I realized a cool thing. The last time I'd been here, just me and my fire and the starry sky, I didn't have to call him. He called me.

"I guess you're already here." I felt dumb saying it out loud, but I said it anyway.

The usual summer noises of crickets and campfire songs weren't there to ward off the lonely silence of Owl Woods. But something clicked, and not just frozen twigs bumping together above my head. What Reece said in her letter about my grounding made all kinds of sense. I was more free when I was grounded than when I was un-grounded. Mom had called me a man for the first time. Dad was proud of me. The police trusted me, and the Stallards were going to follow my lead about the armor of God.

All of a sudden the past few months went rushing past me: from a treasure hunt exploding into a small town mystery to . . . to I didn't know what. A grand plan maybe.

So the truth does set you free. It can be a bumpy ride though. Maybe that's the two-sided meaning of *omen*: sometimes the truth is scary.

There even seemed to be a lesson in the broken compass: following lies will get you nowhere. I felt wise knowing that. So, was I to be the next hotshot in the archaeology world or in the crime-solving world? Since Reece had been saying big prayers for me for a long time, it was as much about her as me.

I stood there in the cold and dark with my eagle-bone whistle, just being quiet.

"You're here?" I asked, and took the wide silence to mean yes.

I looked at the whistle in my hand: "So I don't really need this?" I felt a little guilty, for Reece's sake. "Well," I said, "she gave it to me and I like it a lot. So . . . here's a song I've been working on, in case you want to listen."

I raised the whistle, put it to my mouth and played a melody. It was only a few notes up and down, which I repeated over and over, but I liked it. I played on, clear and high and lonely until my throat tightened up. I had to stop to breathe and work out the lump in my chest.

"That's it," I said when I finished. "Probably not the best thing you've had played for you."

I headed back. My house came into view, and as I ran, it seemed to move toward me through the trees—big and cozy, outlined against the black sky, with little squares of gold light from the windows calling me home. I felt like the luckiest person alive.

"Hey, I'm going to need your help finding the next armor piece," I said, as if he were a friend right by my side. "I have no idea where to start."

I stopped and listened. A word came into my head, deep and quiet strong.

Signs.

"Signs?" I asked.

The word came again. *Signs.*

THE RAVEN'S CURSE

ROBBIE suspected bad times were coming when the biggest raven he'd ever seen took up residence like a weather vane on his raccoon-and-mannequin-infested house—better known as The Castle.

Winter in Ohio was bare and brown—depressing to a kid like me used to the coast and the tropics. We were trudging across Robbie's front yard when this black menace swooped in on the tower and crowed at us: *Wonk! Wonk!*

"Whoa!" I said. "Get a load of that bird!"

Robbie narrowed his big, blue eyes at the bird. It lifted its wings, glided from the rusty roof to a bare tree in the front yard, and tipped its head at us. "Ravens are a sign of bad luck," he said.

I glanced at Elijah, who knew about things in nature. He may not really be Creek Indian like he always hoped, but he's the best I've seen at knowing things about trees and weather and animals: the ways of the wild.

Elijah studied the bird and scanned the sky. "Common raven," he said uneasily. "He's out of his habitat. Ravens stay to mountains and gorges to the north, in New England and Canada." He looked worried about the bird.

Creek's a little strange, but he's all right.

For reasons unknown to us at the time, Elijah Creek was the heart of our search for the armor of God—ancient battle gear full of secrets and histories we were trying to decipher. The rest of us thought we were along for the ride, that's all. We sat there on The Castle's droopy porch under the raven's beady eye, drinking Mrs. Wingate's hot chocolate with whipped cream and cinnamon sprinkles.

"We're at a standstill," Robbie said, wiping whipped cream off his lip.

"No." Reece bundled against the wind. "This is just down time. Look what we've done in one semester: we found the armor of God buried in Old Pilgrim Church . . ."

"And lost it," Robbie said.

"But found the helmet of salvation near the graveyard," she went on firmly.

"Lost it!" Robbie smirked at Elijah, who had done the losing.

"Ancient history," said Reece, defending Elijah. "We did find it. That's my point."

Mei added, "We know it is somewhere, okay? We found the belt of truth. The rest of the armor is close."

"The belt? Let's see now," Robbie tapped his chin, "where could that be . . . oh yeah, lost that too!" He grinned wickedly, as if he were glad the quest was one step forward and two steps back.

I should've noticed Robbie splintering off from the rest of us at that point. Sure, he could be a whiner; but judging how he could throw himself into long, tiring play rehearsals, tons of library research, and even metal detecting in the dead of winter, my guess was he wasn't really spoiled. Maybe, being an only child, he just liked the attention he got from whining. But something else was going on.

Ancient Truth

✖✖

(page 8) "Put on the full armor of God so that you can take your stand against the devil's schemes."

Ephesians 6:11

(page 24) "You will know the truth, and the truth will set you free."

John 8:32

(page 44) "Be still, and know that I am God;
I will be exalted among the nations,
I will be exalted in the earth."

Psalm 46:10

(page 138) "Blessed are the pure in heart, for they will see God."

Matthew 5:8

Creek Code

Japanese
Mei Aizawa—(May I-zawa)
Baka mitai—(bah-kah-mee-tie) That seems crazy
Daijoubu—(die-jo-boo) It's all right
Ganbatte—(gahm-bah-tay) Hang in there
Sugoi—(soo-goy) Wow

Greek
Aletheia—truth
Koinonia—fellowship
Soterion—salvation

Hebrew
(awlef mame noon)—truth, faithfulness

Check out this other new series . . .

GAME ON!

Stephen D. Smith with Lise Caldwell

GAME ON! is a sports fiction series featuring young athletes who must overcome obstacles—on and off the field. The characters in these stories are neither the best athletes nor the underdogs. These are ordinary kids of today's culture—characters you'll identify with and be inspired by.

RED CARD

0-7847-1438-X

RIVALS ON THE WAVES

0-7847-1470-3

HIGH HURDLES

0-7847-1439-8

FOURTH AND LONG

0-7847-1471-1